Genesis

A Soul Savers Novella

Books by Kristie Cook

— SOUL SAVERS SERIES —
www.SoulSaversSeries.com

Promise
Purpose
Devotion (February 2012)

Genesis: A Soul Savers Novella

Find the author at www.KristieCook.com

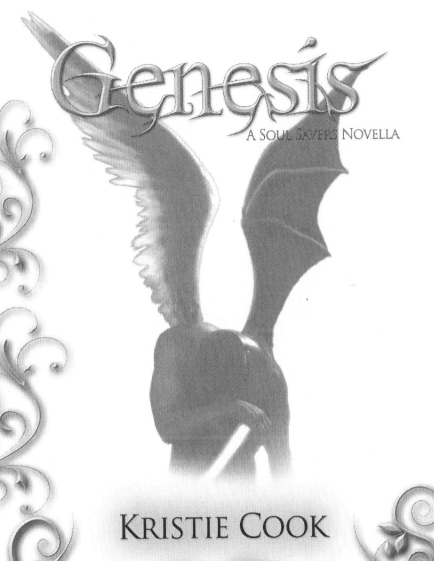

Genesis

A Soul Savers Novella

KRISTIE COOK

Ang'dora Productions, LLC

Naples, Florida

Published by
Ang'dora Productions, LLC
15275 Collier Blvd
#201-300
Naples, FL 34119

Ang'dora Productions and associated logos are trademarks and/
or registered trademarks of Ang'dora Productions, LLC

Cover design by Brenda Pandos

This book is a work of fiction. Names, characters and events
are either products of the author's imagination or are used
fictitiously and any resemblance to actual persons, living or
dead, is entirely coincidental.

ISBN 978-0-9846990-0-1

First Edition October 2011

Printed in the United States of America

For Shawn Cook
In Celebration of 20 Years

Acknowledgements

A million thank-you's go out to all the people who helped Genesis become a reality and ensured I stayed (somewhat) sane along the way.

More appreciation than I can ever put into words go out to my family – Shawn, Zakary, Austin and Nathan, as well as Mom, Terry, Dad and Keena – for your tremendous support, for believing in me, for keeping me motivated and, most of all, for all that you put up with, especially as deadlines barrel my way.

Chrissi Jackson, my publisher, close friend and business partner, thank you for serving as my sounding board, especially when my ideas got really kooky; for holding me up when I felt like falling; and for keeping me focused when my mind soared to far off places. I can't fathom the idea of doing this without you.

Author Brenda Pandos, I can't thank you enough for my gorgeous covers, for your keen eye to my writing mistakes, for pushing me out of my comfort zone, and, most of all, for your friendship. We're doing this, babe, we're really doing it. And we're laughing all the way. Yes, KM for the win!

Author Lani Woodland, author Melonie Piper and Judy Spelbring, thank you for enduring my drafts and providing your insight to make this story as tight and strong as Niko's bod. Author Michelle Gregory and Patti Oaks, thank you for your sharp eyes and for fixing my goofs. Author Jessica Bell, thank you for answering my seemingly endless questions about Greece (you're not off the hook, though—next up is Australia).

Lisa Adams, thank you for all you've done to help keep the chaos under control, both personally and professionally. Tammi, thank you for your friendship, for keeping me grounded in real life and for the laughs on our rides. Jessica and Lisa, a special thank you to you both for your unwavering support, for your love for my books and characters and for all that you do not just for me and other authors, but for the thousands of readers following you.

Readers, my heartfelt appreciation goes out to you all. You make this happen. You keep me going with the beautiful fan mail you send me, with the reviews you post and with the recommendations you pass on to friends, family and even strangers. Without you, all of this would be pointless – just words tucked into a corner of a hard drive, enjoyed only by me. From every cell in my body, from every corner of my world, from the depths of my heart and soul, thank you for reading!

Prologue

The Angel hovered near the veil between the Otherworld and the physical realm, close enough to take a nearly solid form and near enough to the woman he guarded that he could reach out and caress her cheek. But the distance between them may as well have been the distance of the entire universe. Although Andrew could see her clearly through the veil, she couldn't see him and she never would—a fact that pierced his soul with more agony than a demon's blade. He had to ignore that pain, however, as well as his feelings for her.

Andrew could not fathom his love toward this single human. Angels, even warriors such as himself, naturally loved all humans equally—a sacred love only surpassed by their Master's. His many wards over the millennia had never made him feel as this one did, this human woman known as Zoe from the part of Earth called Thessaly. He did not know what made her different, but from the day he became her guardian, his soul ached to be more than an invisible entity in her life. It wanted to be a part of her physical world. But such desire was dangerous. Forbidden.

Human emotions such as these could cast Andrew out of Heaven, deliver him straight into his enemies' hands and transform him into one of the very creatures he was created to conquer. The thought of becoming one of them—the fallen, the demons, Satan's followers—appalled him. He'd rather be extinguished, even if it never meant being a part of Zoe's physical life. He would destroy her as a demon, but he could save her soul as an Angel.

For her sake, he must suppress his feelings and focus on his duties. He needed to remain alert, ready for battle.

The Higher Angels had special plans for Zoe, although they did not share these plans with Andrew. He was a mere warrior, one who followed orders, not one who issued them. His orders were to protect her, to keep her out of the demons' hands and alive at all costs. Orders he gladly followed. He would fight for her soul with unmatched ferocity, and according to his superiors, tonight would be the first battle.

Andrew perched on a boulder, feeling the rock's physicality beneath his not-quite-solid feet, as he watched and waited, his body coiled and ready for the fight. On the other side of the veil, Zoe, unaware of impending danger, knelt by the creek. The moonlight bounced off its rippled surface, washing the color out of her smooth olive skin and casting shadows over her dark brown eyes. She splashed water on her face and glanced up at the half-moon, then suddenly turned her head toward Andrew.

He tensed, for a moment thinking she could see him as her eyes seemed to focus right on him, piercing his soul. If she could, she would see a hard, muscular man with light hair, white wings rising from his bare back, a multitude of weapons hanging from his belt and a long sword in his right hand. Her brows pushed together for the briefest moment and then she let out the saddest sigh he'd ever heard, as if disappointed when she saw nothing but the boulder. Her head dropped and her shoulders sank. Locks of dark hair had escaped the braids wound around her head and now curtained her face as she stared at her lap, her hands twisting into the linen of her tunic.

Andrew heard the noise of someone approaching before Zoe did and sprang to attention. She jumped to her feet, too, and turned toward *him*—a move that could have cost her life. In the physical realm, three men came at her from behind and one quickly pinned her to the ground.

At the same time, a demon charged the Angel in the Otherworld.

Andrew swung his sword up just in time to parry the demon's blade. Another arced toward him and he spun, at the same time releasing a dagger from his belt to block the blow. His silver blade clashed with the black one and a shower of sparks rained down. He landed with bent knees, a weapon in each hand, facing the evil spirit in its physical form.

With horns protruding from its temples, razor-sharp teeth, fiery eyes, talon feet and black wings, the demon looked like the Angel's opposite, though both were hard-bodied warriors conditioned for battle. But while Angels protected human souls, demons sought to destroy them. This one wanted Zoe's. Curling its upper lip in a snarl, it rose higher in the air, held its blade straight out in front and shot like an arrow toward Andrew.

The Angel's feathered wings spread widely and lifted him out of the demon's way. Andrew continued upward, beating his wings harder, as the beast switched directions and came at him again. He dipped and turned and swung his sword, slicing through the demon's thin-skinned wing. It howled with pain and rage and tried to fly at Andrew again. Instead of crashing into him, however, the injured wing sent the beast careening to his right. As it soared by, its arm jabbed out with full strength, knocking Andrew in the chest.

As he tumbled in the air with the blow, he caught sight of Zoe struggling against the man who pinned her to the ground. Andrew knew the three figures weren't quite human, but were Satan's minions, part of his army in the physical world. Zoe would only see three men attacking her. Although they might rape her, they really thirsted for her human blood. Andrew could do nothing about them, however. His purpose was to fight off this demon, driving it away from her soul. He couldn't be distracted by the physical realm. He had to focus on his own battle and hope Zoe would win hers.

Andrew regained control and now took the offensive. Holding his sword and dagger out in front of him, he charged at the demon, aiming for its chest. The beast swung both of its swords out and locked the Angel's blades between them. Still gripping the hilts tightly, Andrew flipped over its head and yanked his weapons free. A demon blade pulled loose, too, flying back and carving a gash into Andrew's thigh. He grimaced as gold blood spurted from the wound. The sweet scent threw the demon into a frenzy.

The two flew at each other and became a blur of tangled limbs and clashing blades. The demon bit with fangs, slashed with talons and sliced with swords, shredding the Angel's form. Andrew had never faced such a powerful opponent—tonight he might suffer his first loss in two millennia—but he refused to give up easily. He tore into the demon's thick hide with every swing of his weapons. Splatters of both black blood and gold dotted their faces and bodies.

When Zoe's screams fell silent, the Angel glanced into the physical realm. Her still body lay on the ground, her dark hair and eyes—staring blind and empty—contrasting with the new paleness of her face. The three figures stood over her with blood-stained lips. At the neckline of Zoe's tunic, a tiny crimson flower bloomed with the smallest trickle of blood leaking from her throat. They had consumed the rest.

Andrew screamed a protest and his face contorted with rage as he turned to the demon. The evil one lifted the corners of its mouth as if in a grin. Andrew crossed his blades over his head. His wings beat a hard rhythm against the air as he gathered his power and channeled it to the swords. Then with all his might and energy, he swung the blades down and out, slicing through the demon's neck. Black blood rained over the Angel as the head fell from its body.

Andrew wished he could have killed the evil beast, ended its existence forever, but that was no more possible than the demon being able to kill him. They could be injured to the point of incapacitation, ending that particular battle, but neither would ever die. They were spirits, denizens of the Otherworld since the beginning of time and into eternity. With a growl of defeat, the beast collapsed over its head and its physical form disintegrated into nothing.

Andrew returned his attention to Zoe. He'd saved her soul, but those creatures still appeared intent on taking what remained of her life. Through the veil, he heard them discussing whether to let her die or to turn her into one of them, the vile beasts that were no better than the demons themselves. One lifted Zoe off the ground by her neck, her head hanging unnaturally to the side.

Andrew bellowed with rage and flew at the men.

He knocked into their stone-like, inhuman bodies and they tumbled onto each other in a heap. Zoe fell and Andrew dove out to catch her. The men stared at him with wide eyes the same color as the blood that still pooled around their teeth as their mouths gaped open.

The Angel
    had crossed
        the veil.

He'd left the Otherworld and entered the physical realm. Terror filled the men's eyes and they disappeared with three popping sounds.

Alone, Andrew lowered Zoe's lifeless body to the ground and cradled her head in his lap. His now solid form ached and throbbed with its many cuts and gashes. He needed to return to the Otherworld, to the Heavens, to heal, but looking down at Zoe's still face, he had no thought for himself. Pearl-like tears dropped onto her pale cheek. She'd lost much blood, probably too much to survive, but her precious heart still beat, the sound slow and faint.

I can save her.

It was a dangerous thought. One he shouldn't even be considering. But Andrew couldn't bear a future without his beloved Zoe to watch over anymore. And the Higher Angels had told him to guard her life at all costs. If he didn't do this, she would surely die.

With that justification, he pulled a small knife from his belt. The demon-inflicted wounds were tainted with the beast's essence, so Andrew gripped the blade and slashed across his wrist, opening a clean wound. Then he held his arm to Zoe's mouth, letting the gold liquid pour into her body. Within a moment, her lips parted on their own.

"Sweet, like honey," she mumbled between swallows, her voice distant and her eyes still closed.

When he felt her essence strengthen, he pulled his wrist away. He knew a taste of his blood would heal her completely. Any more than that, however, he didn't know the potential consequences. Indeed, Angels weren't supposed to share their blood with humans. In fact, they weren't supposed to expose themselves at all unless ordered, which was rare.

Yet . . . here he was.

Zoe's eyes fluttered open and filled with wonder as she gazed up at him, a thrill that made his physical heart pound in his chest. The corners of her full lips pulled into a vague smile. She reached her hand up toward his face.

"So beautiful," she murmured, her voice soft and pure. Aching for her touch, he leaned closer to her fingers, anticipating their caress. But just as her fingertips brushed his skin, he was yanked away from her, out of her realm.

Andrew lost his physical form as he was pulled deeper and deeper through the Otherworld and into the Heavens.

They had no need for words here, unlike the humans. Communication passed through their spirits and Andrew could feel the others' disappointed shock as he soared past them. His spirit came to an abrupt halt when he reached those who'd summoned him: the Higher Angels. They were more than disappointed and surprised. Anger filled their energies.

"You broke several of our laws," came one accusation pulsing through his spirit.

"You let yourself be seen," said another.

"You shared your blood with a human!" This reverberation shook the Heavens with a ferociousness rarely felt here.

"You told me to protect her at all costs," Andrew protested. "She would have died!"

He didn't know if his justification was enough to satisfy them, but it was all he had. The Higher Angels' energy quieted around him, growing into a deafening silence.

"That is the only reason you will be forgiven," a Higher Angel finally said. "This woman is important to our Lord's plans. We can overlook this blasphemy. However . . ."

And the accusation that came next pierced Andrew's soul.

"You love this woman. Not an Angel's love, not spiritual, but a physical love."

He couldn't deny it. He couldn't excuse it. It was true.

"For this you must leave."

"No!" Andrew cried out.

"Your love for her has already caused you to break our laws. What else would you sacrifice for this woman? *Who* would you sacrifice for her?"

Andrew had no response. He didn't know how far he would go for Zoe, but he'd just proven he would violate his commandments. He was a warrior and an Angel—he should have been above such human emotions and rash decisions. His energy swirled as his love for Zoe battled against the shame he felt.

"You cannot stay!" a Higher Angel bellowed. "You must pay for your sin! OUT!"

Sovereign energy blasted at him and he felt the finality of the command. The realization of what it meant swept through him: Fallen Angels were no longer Angels at all.

"Please, no," he implored. "I cannot be a demon. Please don't send me to Satan. I beg of you!"

The energy surrounding him slowed and quieted as the anger dissipated once again. Whispers filled the space as the Higher Angels considered his plea, discussing among themselves. He felt a sense of excitement pass through them, as if an answer they'd been seeking had finally come. He dared to hope this meant they would save him.

"No, you are not of demon essence," the main speaker finally said. "Your sin is love—not hate, not pride, not greed or worse. You are not cursed to the demon world."

Andrew's energy relaxed. But only for a moment. The Higher Angels had not finished.

"You are sentenced to live in the physical realm."

Immediately he felt the pull. His spirit was jerked out of the Heavens and back through the Otherworld, toward the

Earthly realm. He took physical form again, solidifying as he neared the veil. His soul felt split in two. He wanted to be in Zoe's physical world, but not at this price. Never at the cost of losing his wings. His power. His ability to defend her. Who would protect Zoe's soul if he could not?

As he crossed the veil, he heard the Angels' final words.

"For two hundred human years, Andrew, you will live as a man."

Two hundred years. As a man. The words echoed in his physical mind as he fell into the human world. And into complete darkness.

Chapter 1

200 Years Later

Cassandra picked her way through the sea of broken and
battered bodies, the blood-soaked grass squishing under her
sandals. She tried to ignore the warm wetness seeping between
her toes as she searched for signs of life. She doubted she would
find any. This skirmish had been short and vicious, the number
of soldiers on either side not nearly as large as other battlefields
she'd come upon—the Romans, Greeks and Macedonians had
been fighting for as long as she could remember. She hadn't seen
any nearby camps in recent days and assumed these two groups
had surprised each other while en route to joining their legions.

She'd heard the fighting while gathering berries this
morning and waited several hours for it to end, listening—she
could never watch the viciousness—with a knotted stomach as
the last few surrendered. She then waited more hours for the
field to clear as the survivors took their injured comrades with

them and left the rest for dead. But she knew from experience there may be a few she could still help and so, even as twilight approached, she searched.

To her right, one soldier's chest barely lifted and fell and she quickly knelt by his side. His head and unlined face were covered with dark hair and beard, both streaked with crimson, which pooled under his temple. His eyes remained closed. When she lifted his hand by the wrist, he didn't stir. His heartbeat came slow and faint under her fingers and her shoulders sagged with grief. He'd be dead in a matter of minutes, too far gone for her to heal. With tears stinging her brown eyes, she stood and continued searching.

She wound her way across the battlefield, her heart sinking further with each body she passed. Occasionally she stopped to feel for a heartbeat or breath on her hand, but found none. Then, as she stepped over one dead man, another moved. Just barely—just a twitch of his finger. Cassandra hurried to his side. *Please, God, let there be at least someone I can help.*

He was young, barely more than a boy, with black hair and darkly tanned skin, as if he worked in the fields. When Cassandra's eyes traveled over his body, her stomach clenched. The lower half twisted at such unnatural angles, it sickened even her, who'd seen the worst of injuries. She pulled a berry from the pouch hanging at her hip, squished it and slipped it into the young man's mouth. It would help alleviate the pain until death took over.

With a heart that felt like a boulder in her chest, she reached the other side and turned to look out at the field. She swallowed the sob in her throat and scrubbed at her wet cheeks. She'd seen similar scenes over the years, but she never became used to all the carnage. She blew out a sigh heavy with grief and turned to head back to where she currently called home. As she stepped past the last body, only steps from entering the woods, a hand grabbed her ankle.

"Oh!" she cried out and fell to her knees next to a soldier covered in mud and blood. *I almost missed him!* He looked at her with half-closed eyes the color of green olives. He stirred, as if to sit up, but she held him down. "Don't move. Let me see how badly you're hurt first."

"It's just my leg," he said, his voice rough. He pushed himself up onto an elbow, despite her protests. "And my throat. I'm so thirsty."

She pulled a skin of water out of her pouch and handed it to him.

"What is your name?" she asked as she began assessing his condition.

Sweat mixed with dirt smudged his face, but it looked otherwise unscathed, except for a small scratch on his lip and a scrape across his chin. She pushed his dark brown hair back and found a lump on his head. She removed the protective forearm braces and found bruises covering his arms, but no open wounds. His legs had been protected with braces from ankle to knee. Gingerly, she pulled his chiton up just enough to reveal a deep gash in his lower thigh.

After draining the water skin dry, he finally answered. "Niko."

"You're very lucky, Niko," she said, pulling out another skin of water to clean the wound. Then she retrieved a bundle of cut plants from her bag and spread them on her lap. She selected the ones she needed and tore the leaves, then pressed them into the wound. The soldier sucked his breath through clenched teeth. "You seem to be the only man alive here and with barely any injuries, at that."

"Luck has nothing to do with it," he said. "It's all about skill. And I am quite skilled."

She looked up at his face and her herbs seemed to be already working because he managed a confident grin, causing a patch of dried mud to crack around his eye. With a spare piece of cloth soaked with water, she began cleaning his face, trying to ignore how his eyes never left hers. Each swipe of the cloth revealed more of his true appearance and by the time she reached his full lips and square chin, her hand trembled and heat crept into her face. Hiding under the grime was the most handsome man she'd ever seen.

Her eyes dropped, skimming over his strong, warrior's build and she blushed even harder. She was used to looking at soldiers' bodies, assessing them for injuries, touching and prodding them. But now, for the first time, she saw more than a subject to heal. She saw someone who made her heart race and her stomach do odd little flips. And now she felt shy looking at him at all.

"Your hair," he said, lifting his hand. She flinched and her fingers flew to the braids on the sides of her head. His hand fell. "It's just . . . I've never seen such a beautiful color. Like a chestnut."

She swallowed, her throat suddenly dry. Then she hurriedly began gathering her supplies, unable to remain under his gaze any longer. *What's happening to me?*

"I'd better be going," she mumbled.

"Please, don't," Niko said, but then he sighed. "Forgive me. You probably have a husband to return to."

She didn't look up at him. She couldn't stand for her stomach to flip anymore, an absurd reaction she didn't understand. And she couldn't deny his words, although she didn't have a husband. She'd always admired the love her father and mother had shared, but never thought it possible for herself. According to her brother, most girls were married off by their fathers to men they'd never met. Father had no reason or desire to do that to her, though. He believed she would find the right man for herself when the time was right, just as Mother had found him. But she'd never even met a man properly—only those injured and dying on the battlefield, not exactly the appropriate time and place for romantic thoughts. So how could she possibly be having them now?

Niko's assumption made sense, though. She appeared to be the age of a young wife who should be bearing children, but she was actually much, much older. Her explanation for not being married yet would make no sense to this stranger.

"Those herbs will heal the cut," she said, evading his comment. "You'll be fine by morning."

He sat up all the way and she sucked in a breath. *Maybe not.* A bloodstain blossomed down the side of his torn tunic. He'd been lying on it, so she hadn't seen it before.

"You're bleeding," she said.

He looked down and frowned. "I don't feel anything."

He gripped his chiton at the neck and tore it in half, letting the pieces drape over the belt at his waist. She inhaled sharply again. Not at the injury—a superficial scratch—but at his muscular chest and torso. Trying to ignore the pounding of her heart and the quivering in her belly, she cleaned the wound and smeared an herbal paste over it, his eyes on her again the entire time. A pleasant tingling ran through her fingertips and up her arm when she touched him, and when he sighed, not a sound of pain but of pleasure, she wondered if he felt it, too. By the time she finished, her hand trembled once again. Overwhelmed with these inexplicable feelings—*why him?*—she sprang to her feet to leave.

The sound of movement froze her in place. The sun had nearly set and she could barely see the shadows of two men as they approached the far side of the battlefield.

"Could be the Romans," Niko whispered. He staggered to his feet and, in no condition to fight again, limped several paces into the dark woods, gesturing at Cassandra to follow.

They peered around a boulder and watched the men, who apparently hadn't noticed them, as they slowly picked their way through the dead bodies, just as Cassandra had done. Not healers looking for signs of life, though, nor Roman soldiers. They must have been savages here to pillage the bodies.

They stopped at the man with the dark hair and beard who had barely been breathing. They crouched next to him and exchanged words too low for her to hear. Then one bent closer, held his hand over the dying man's mouth and seemed to whisper into his ear. The soldier's arms flailed and his body bucked, as if in pain.

Cassandra gasped. Niko clamped his hand over her mouth.

"They're giving him a quicker death," he whispered in her ear. "Putting him out of his misery."

Before long, the soldier fell limp against the other man, who wiped the inside of his forearm across his mouth, then held it to the dead man's lips. Cassandra peered at Niko, whose brows knitted together, looking just as perplexed as she felt. After several moments, the two men stood and found the only other person who'd shown any signs of life—the youth with the twisted body. This time the second man stooped down and pressed his mouth against the boy's ear. Or was it his throat? Cassandra couldn't discern in the darkness. The youth reacted the same way as the first. They repeated their unusual ritual, then the two men left the way they'd come, leaving any loot behind.

"I've never seen—" Cassandra started to say, but couldn't put words to what they'd just witnessed. It was too strange.

"Perhaps it's a local tradition to send the dead down the River Styx," Niko said. "I've never seen it before. But, I've never been left at the field for dead, either."

She looked up at him. "How could your comrades leave you anyway? They couldn't have thought you dead."

He shrugged. "I think I was unconscious, so perhaps they thought I was. I remember a blow to my head . . . and then you standing next to me. But my men will be back, very soon I'm sure. I'll be fine until then. As much as I'd rather you not, you should probably go home, before darkness falls completely."

Cassandra pursed her lips together, internally debating whether to leave him or not, then finally nodded. After giving Niko her last skins of water and receiving more assurances from him that he'd be fine, she hurried through the woods and across the fields in the twilight. She thought Father would be worried, but he was already asleep by the time she walked through the door of their hut. They had lived like nomads her entire life, always in the wilderness, sometimes in caves, sometimes in huts built by Father. He was a strong, vibrant man and usually didn't turn in so early. *He must have had a long day. He's just tired.* She refused to think it could be anything else.

She tended the fire to keep them warm for the night and ate the last of the morning's bread with the berries she'd collected before she'd come upon the battlefield. She hoped Jordan, her brother, would return with supplies soon—they had enough grain and oil for only another day or two. She lay down in her bed of furs and stared at the fire without seeing it. Niko's face filled her vision.

She worried about him in the woods by himself, injured. She told herself it was a minor injury and he was a soldier, that he could take care of himself. *His men will find him. He's fine. Stop thinking about him.* She finally dozed off but slept fitfully. Dreams of wild animals and Roman soldiers attacking Niko haunted her sleep. She awoke before dawn and knew, before she even opened her eyes, she would go back to check on him.

Father still snored and she took advantage of the opportunity to sneak out and back to the battlefield. She followed the light of the full moon that still hung high in the sky, skirting the woods this time. The darkness within them frightened her. Animals would be on the hunt and from the sounds, not all were small creatures. The cracks of large branches breaking made her believe something in there was big enough to eat her. But she refused to turn back. Her concern for Niko outweighed her fear.

When she approached the tree she'd left him under, though, her heart sank. He was nowhere around. She took a few timid steps farther into the woods, peering into the darker areas where he might have found better shelter, but no sign of him existed at all. Not even blood or any indication of a struggle.

She blew out an exasperated breath. After hours of nightmares and little sleep, she'd worried for nothing. His comrades must have returned and taken him back to their camp. Relief that he was safe finally washed through her, followed by a twinge of disappointment. She'd been hoping, more than she'd realized, she'd see him again.

She looked out at the battlefield, expecting to find fewer bodies. If they'd come for Niko, surely they'd taken their dead, as well. But the shadows of the bodies in the pre-dawn darkness seemed to show the same scene she'd left last evening. *Then they'll be returning soon.* Which meant she needed to leave.

As she turned, someone in the middle of the battlefield suddenly sat up. A surprised gasp escaped her throat and the man turned his head toward her, the moon's light illuminating his face. Her eyes widened. She recognized him: the dark bearded man the other two had mercifully killed.

As he stood up, so did another. The boy. The one whose legs and back had been so twisted and broken, he couldn't possibly be alive. But there he stood.

Both soldiers sniffed the air in her direction and let out a feral growl. Then they started toward her, their legs and bodies jerking clumsily, as if re-learning how to walk.

Cassandra's throat worked hard to swallow the lump in it. "Can I . . . can I help you?"

They continued lurching toward her. As they came closer and she could see their faces more clearly, her heart raced even harder. Instead of brown or green or any normal eye color, theirs were red. And *glowing*.

"Thirsty," the boy said, his voice too old and broken for such a young face.

"Need . . . blood," the man croaked. His hand clutched at his throat while the other reached out, as if to grasp her shoulder though they were still several paces away.

Hunger flared in both of their eyes and their upper lips lifted, revealing teeth that looked more like an animal's than a human's.

Cassandra cried out. Then she spun around and ran.

Their halting footsteps pounded behind her. She imagined feeling their ragged breaths on her neck, though she had too much of a lead to truly feel it. But her peplos slowed her down, the ankle-length tunic twisting around her legs. She glanced over her shoulder once. The soldiers were gaining on her, their awkwardness seeming to fall away with each step they took.

Not caring how inappropriate it was, she hitched the bottom of her peplos to her thighs, freeing her legs. She dug her feet into the ground and sprang forward as hard as she could. She knew she ran faster than most people—speed was one of her family's unusual abilities—but she couldn't outrun these . . . these undead men.

A hand brushed against her shoulder and she screamed. She cut sharply to her right and tore through the woods, forgetting her earlier fear of the beasts that roamed within. She had worse worries now. She thought. Something crashed through the trees to her right. She glanced over to see yellow eyes and a mouth of sharp teeth bounding through the woods next to her, keeping her pace. It suddenly veered left, cutting her off.

She skidded to a halt, dirt and leaves spraying in the air. A wolf taller than her stood in her path, its hackles raised and its lips pulled back from teeth longer than her index finger. Its yellow eyes burned into her with a wild hunger and a line of drool hung from its fang. The two men . . . creatures . . . whatever they were . . . slowed their steps behind her, whether because they feared the wolf or thought they had her trapped, she didn't know.

The animal growled. The men hissed. Cassandra spun to her left and took off running again. She broke through the edge of the woods into a clearing near home, jaws snapping right behind her. The sky had lightened considerably with the coming dawn but, looking over her shoulder at the three beasts chasing her, she didn't see the looming figure in front of her. She grunted with the collision, the body hard and unmoving as she slammed into it.

Chapter 2

"*Cassandra?*" Jordan barked, grabbing his sister by the shoulders just as she plowed into him. He'd dropped everything when he heard the crashing through the woods, but hadn't expected his sister to be the one making all the noise. Then two men and an unusually large wolf broke through the tree line, all of their eyes full of hunger and lust. Jordan pushed Cassandra behind him and drew out his sword.

The wolf halted in its tracks. Its yellow eyes locked with Jordan's and a strange feeling the wolf somehow knew him brushed the back of his mind. With a thunderous growl, the beast suddenly turned and lunged at the men, hitting one and knocking him to the ground. The other soldier grabbed the wolf's neck and threw it to the side. Jordan's brow lifted at the display of inhuman strength. *Impressive.* The wolf snarled again and attacked the second man. He raised his arm in defense and the animal's snout latched on. The three became a snarling, growling and hissing ball of swinging arms and snapping jaws.

Jordan grabbed Cassandra's upper arm and lifted her to her feet. As they slowly backed away, the sun edged above the horizon, flooding the clearing with its brightness, and the fight ceased immediately. All three of the combatants looked to the sky. The men cringed and their hands flew up to shield their red eyes, while the wolf whimpered and ran away. The men's bodies sagged, as if suddenly and completely exhausted. They exchanged a puzzled glance before loping off into the darker woods. Jordan noticed how neither of them had a single scratch or any blood from the wolf's teeth or claws.

"Let's go," he whispered, still staring after the strange men. He wanted to chase after them—to find out who or *what* they were—but Cassandra still trembled at his side. "Come on."

She ran as though she were still being chased. Jordan followed on her heels, resisting the urge to pass her, staying behind just in case the others came back. They flew into the hut and slammed the door behind them.

"Father!" Cassandra gasped between pants as she braced the door with a stripped tree limb. "Father, you'll never believe—"

Jordan clasped her wrist, breaking her off. He felt her eyes on him, questioning, but he couldn't stop his own stare to look at her. Father lay sprawled on the dirt floor, nowhere near his bedding, his hair—blond and shoulder-length, just like Jordan's—curtaining his face. Cassandra lunged to his side, falling to her knees, but Jordan remained frozen with shock, fearing the worst. *He can't die. It's . . . impossible.*

"Father?" his sister said, shaking him. "Father, what happened?"

Father blinked several times and then his eyes finally focused on her. Jordan blew out the breath he hadn't realized he'd been holding and finally found the ability to move. He knelt beside them.

"I don't know," Father whispered. "I believe I am not well."

Jordan's brow furrowed as Father struggled to stand on shaky legs. None of them had ever been sick, not even Father. They hardly even aged. But now that Jordan looked at him more closely, he noticed lines around Father's eyes that hadn't been there the last time he'd been home, only weeks ago. Even the color of his eyes—they once shared the same deep blue—seemed lighter and distant, as if he already gazed into another place. As if he'd already left them.

How could this be! A hot seed planted itself in Jordan's stomach—a seed of anger.

"You should stay in bed today," Cassandra said to Father, her voice muffled by the blood whirring in Jordan's ears. "You just need some rest."

Lost in his own angry thoughts, Jordan watched as Cassandra slid her arm around Father's waist and helped him make the few steps to his bedding. As he collapsed into a heap and Cassandra tended to him, a memory of Mother flashed before Jordan's eyes—she'd looked just the same right before she died decades ago.

He needed air.

Despite his sister's protests, he fled outside with the excuse of retrieving the goods he'd brought home. He took his time crossing the clearing and distracted himself by thinking of the men and the wolf. If they had returned, they hadn't discovered his haul. He cocked his head to listen for them, but only heard birds chirping from the treetops and the sounds of small rodents rustling in the leaves of the forest floor. He considered how all three of them had stopped when the sun hit them and then retreated. His eyes narrowed with a thought . . . .

But he didn't have time to think now. If he delayed too long, Cassandra would come looking for him and the ingredients she needed for Father's soup.

While she cooked, she told them the whole story.

"Dead bodies stood up and walked?" Father asked, his voice sounding stronger but bewildered. "Cassandra, what kind of berries have you been eating?"

Jordan snorted. Cassandra put one hand on her hip and waved her spoon at Father, her chin jutting out as it always did when they teased her.

"I know my edibles. You know that. I saw what I saw and it was terrifying."

Yes, Cassandra knew her edibles and Jordan knew she'd been truly frightened. But dead men walking? Absurd.

"It *was* very strange," he conceded. "They didn't appear to be normal men, I can agree with that."

"That wolf wasn't normal either," Cassandra said.

Jordan didn't respond, but stroked his chin as he gazed into the fire. She was right. The wolf *wasn't* normal. The way it had looked at him—as if some human awareness existed behind the yellow eyes. Jordan shook himself. *It was just an animal.* But his curiosity was piqued. He wished he had chased after them.

"Did they follow you home?" Father asked and the alarm in his voice caught Jordan's attention.

Cassandra shook her head. "I don't believe so. They disappeared into the woods and I don't think anyone has *ever* run as fast as we did."

"Well, you do get your speed from me," Father said with a chuckle that broke down into a fit of coughing.

Cassandra threw Jordan a worried look. The hot seed within him sprouted and his anger grew again. Father was truly ill, possibly even dying. *This can't happen!* It went against everything Jordan believed in. And if Father died . . . all of Jordan's plans would die along with him. The anger sparked hotter.

"Why were you out before the sun rose?" he demanded of Cassandra, trying to distract himself from this sudden anger. She glanced over at Father, who appeared to have fallen back to sleep, and then she turned away, as if to hide her pink face. She began putting away the goods he'd brought home.

"I helped a soldier after a battle last night. I was worried about him so I went back to where I—" She cut herself off with a gasp and turned to Jordan with wide brown eyes. "What if those . . . those *things* got to him? Maybe that's why I couldn't find him."

Jordan narrowed his eyes. Cassandra had always been the compassionate one. She'd inherited their mother's healing skills and couldn't stay off a battlefield, even when she should be home where she belonged. So her concern didn't surprise him. But he heard something else in her voice that he didn't like, fueling his anger. He drew in a deep breath.

"How badly was he injured?" he finally asked, trying to sound sincere with his concern.

"Just some cuts and a lump on the head. I thought his comrades had come back for him, but . . . Jordan, what if . . . ?"

She swallowed hard and fear filled her eyes. She seemed to care more for this soldier than any others. That's what he'd sensed from her just a moment ago. Why did it irritate him so much? He didn't know. But he did know this gave him an excuse to get out of that hut. Away from their dying father. Away from his annoying sister. And a chance to hunt down those strange creatures. He started gathering his weapons.

"I'll go search for him and see."

"You can't go out there. It's too dangerous!"

One side of his mouth pulled into a lop-sided grin. At least she still cared about him.

"Don't worry about me, little sister," he said. "This will be fun!"

He was through the door before she could stop him—or throw anything at him. She hated it when he called her "little sister," because she was, in fact, a few minutes older than him. He liked to tease her, though, because he towered over her tiny body with his tall, muscular build.

He felt free as soon as he left the confines of the tiny hut.

He sucked in a deep draw of air and blew it out, then sprinted for the woods.

Cassandra's pursuers had left clear enough paths of their retreats. The men's footprints led in the same direction as Cassandra had said the battlefield was, but the wolf had gone a separate way. More interested in the wolf, Jordan followed the large paw prints.

He couldn't shake the feeling he had made some kind of connection with the animal. Why had it looked at him so ... intelligently? Why had it backed off when it saw him? Did the wolf feel the darkness in Jordan, the darkness that had been deepening and growing for years, making him feel isolated from the rest of his family? But it hadn't feared his darkness as many animals—and humans—did when they sensed it. The wolf had almost seemed to protect him, changing its target from his sister and him to those two strange men.

Jordan growled at himself. *It's just a wolf. An animal. And I'll slay it for making my thoughts sound like a madman's.* He quickened his pace.

The wolf prints eventually circled back toward the battlefield, but just as the trees began thinning at the woods' edge, all evidence of the animal disappeared. No more paw prints. No fur caught on tree bark or low branches.

Jordan searched in a widening circle but all he eventually found, near a boulder only a few paces inside the woods, were human footprints. *From Cassandra's soldier?* He peered out at the battlefield, where a dozen men carried their fallen comrades to a pile on the far side. Her soldier must be with them. *Well, he's safe now.* As if he really cared.

He returned to where the wolf's prints had left off but still found no trace. Frustrated, Jordan headed home and the closer he came, the more his anger at Father grew. The old man owed them answers. If Father was truly dying, he needed to explain himself—and everything about them—something he had refused to do all these years.

Jordan had developed countless theories, but the one that made the most sense—they were descendants of the gods everyone else believed in—conflicted with their own beliefs in one God. Cassandra rarely played his game of hypothesizing, telling him they should simply be grateful for the blessings God had given them. Of course, unlike him, she'd been kept from associating with other people—women didn't belong in public places—so she didn't fully understand just how different they were. How much better they were than all others.

"How is he?" Jordan demanded as soon as he burst into the hut.

Cassandra sat on the floor, next to Father's sleeping form, her eyes wide and her body tense with the sudden intrusion. She blinked, then her eyes narrowed.

"You're back already? What did you find?"

"Nothing," he growled. "How is he?"

"Did you even look?"

"There were soldiers in the field, gathering their dead. I didn't find anyone in the woods, so I'm sure he's with them." Jordan nodded at the sleeping form next to her. "What about our father? Shouldn't *he* be your concern?"

Her shoulders sagged, as did the corners of her mouth.

"Nothing I do is working. He's been sleeping, but fitfully, crying out every now and then. Mostly Mother's name, but sometimes other things. But it's all nonsense."

Jordan removed his weapons and tossed them onto his bedding. He knelt on Father's far side, across from his sister. "He must come around. He needs to explain—"

Cassandra was already shaking her head and Father, as if anticipating Jordan's demand, silenced him.

"I . . . must . . . tell them," Father croaked. "It is time."

He fell silent again. Jordan exchanged looks with his sister, but she just shook her head. She brushed Father's hair from his forehead, away from his closed eyes.

"Hush, Father. Do not—"

The old man's eyelids sprang open and he glared at her with full alertness. "Yes. I *must* tell you. You need to know."

He tried to rise, struggling to sit up. Jordan gathered more blankets and pelts and propped him up as much as possible. Father's face looked haggard and his eyes pale and red-rimmed as they rested first on Jordan and then on Cassandra. He licked his cracked lips and closed his eyes. When he began, his voice suddenly came as clear and as strong as it always had.

"Your mother and I have told you the story of how we met," he said. "How I remembered nothing of my life before. I've always said it was as though I'd never lived in this world until the moment I met her." He opened his eyes and pierced them with his blue gaze. "Which, my dear children, is actually quite true."

Jordan sat back on his heels as he listened to his father's story, which felt so real and true the way he told it, but could not be possible. When Father was done, he closed his eyes again and sagged against the mound of blankets.

"I have told them. They know now," he murmured, obviously no longer talking to them.

Cassandra looked at Jordan and he looked back at her with lifted brows.

"That's it?" Jordan asked with incredulity. "All this time we've wanted to know what made us different from everyone else, and that's his explanation?"

Jordan teetered on the edge of exploding. Cassandra shook her head violently. "Jordan, he's very ill. He's just delirious."

"I would say so! What does he think we are? *Children?* Infants who believe in such nonsense?"

"Please, Jordan—"

Her plea for him to calm down was cut off by a gasp from Father's lips. He gripped their hands with unexpected strength.

"You ... must ... *believe*," he said, desperation filling his voice.

"How are we supposed to believe such a story?" Jordan demanded. His own theories had never been this outlandish. He'd always believed both Father and Mother were human— perhaps descendants of something greater, but still human. But what Father just said ...

Suddenly Jordan could see nothing around him. Cassandra, Father and the entire hut disappeared, his vision taken over by strange images that were not his own. He saw a white-winged Angel who looked just like his father battling a demon with thin, black membranes for wings and horns protruding from its head. He also saw their mother lying unconscious on the bank of a stream. Then Father defeated the demon and fell to their mother's side. He watched it all play out, the same story Father had just told them. Then just as abruptly as it had disappeared, the hut returned.

"What was that?" Jordan demanded. "Cass, did you see that, too?"

She blinked at him, her face twisted in a mix of emotions—the same wonder, disbelief and confusion he felt. She nodded. They both looked at Father. The corners of his lips lifted in the slightest of smiles.

"Just one of my abilities. I had to share." He rose from his bed then, too strong for even Jordan to restrain. He rose above them both, until his head touched the ceiling. Jordan's jaw fell as he watched thin, black wings spread from Father's back, reaching the walls on both sides yet still not fully extended while his body seemed to fade into a dark shadow. "It is time for me to go."

Chapter 3

Cassandra stared at Father, her mouth hanging open while bittersweet tears scalded her cheeks. She never thought she would lose him, convinced he would live forever after so many years as a strong and youthful man, but she knew he was about to leave her now. What would she do without him? Jordan liked his adventures too much to stay with her and she could never go with him—not that he'd even take her. She would be on her own now. How she would miss Father's heavenly voice when he sang while they gathered fruits and olives, and their fireside conversations that could last for several nights. Her heart ached as sharp blades of grief and loneliness already stabbed it.

But at the same time, she could feel Father's joy. He emanated a happiness she hadn't felt in him since Mother died.

And he was so beautiful and glorious! Great white, feathered wings spread from his back, touching the walls, and his skin shone, bathed in a warm light. *This is his true self. He's going where he belongs.* As much as Cassandra wanted to keep him for herself, she had to let him go.

"I love you, Father," she whispered.

"I love you, too, my daughter," he said and he looked at Jordan. "And I love you, my son. You have dark days ahead of you, but please remember that I always loved you and I always will." Father fell silent and cocked his head. "It is time. Time for me to be with your mother."

He reached out for their hands and Jordan recoiled but Cassandra grasped Father's hand, feeling warmth and love travel through her arm. Father gave her a squeeze, closed his eyes and, as if murmuring to himself, said, "I am coming, Zoe."

His wings beat the air twice and then he disappeared. Another vision filled Cassandra's mind: Father and Mother walking along the seashore hand-in-hand, one of Father's wings stretched protectively around Mother.

While Cassandra's heart broke into pieces, her lips pulled into a smile. *They're together again.*

A loud crash yanked her back to full awareness.

Her head jerked to the right. The water skin Jordan had been holding sat in the middle of the remains of a pottery bowl. She turned back to him, her mouth opening to question him but she snapped it shut. Her brother's eyes flared and his mouth twisted with anger.

"He tells us that," he spewed, "shows us . . . *that* . . . and then *leaves?*"

Cassandra stood and stepped closer to him. She reached for his hands, but he jerked them away. Her hands fell to her side. "He's happy now, Jordan. He's with Mother again. They're in a better place."

"A *better* place? Where do you think they are? Demons do *not* go to Heaven, little sister."

Cassandra flinched as if he'd just slapped her. "Demons? What are you talking about?"

"A fallen Angel is a demon. Father himself taught us that and he was a fallen Angel."

"No—"

"You saw him just now. Black wings and horns on his head!"

Cassandra shook her head. "He *fought* the demon, Jordan. Father was the Angel."

"And then he fell. You saw that, too, right? He fell from the Heavens. They cast him out." Jordan clenched his teeth so hard, his jaw twitched. "And just now—as he rose like a demon in front of our eyes, with those thin, black wings and talons and horns . . ."

Cassandra gasped. "No! Beautiful, white, feathered wings. He's an Angel. He's gone back!"

Jordan glared at her as if she were a fool who didn't understand what was so obvious to him, which she really didn't. *Black wings? Talons and horns? What had Jordan seen?*

He turned his back on her and crouched beside the fire. He stared at the low flames licking at the cypress wood, and his shoulders rose as he inhaled slowly, as if trying to calm a different fire—one she could feel burning inside him, just below the surface. She didn't like him when he was like this. He'd always had a dark side the rest of her family did not and it scared her when it surfaced. When he spoke, however, he didn't yell or curse at her. Rather, his voice came low and deliberate, which she found even more disturbing.

"He's gone to Hell, Cassandra. Accept it. He was an Angel. He's *now* a demon." He stood again and turned toward her, darkness filling his face and fire in his eyes. "And so are we."

Her hand flew to her throat. Her own voice came out in a rough whisper. "Jordan . . . how can you—"

"We are of his blood. His demon blood runs through our veins. That's why we age so slowly, why we run so fast and can lift fallen trees three times our body weight. We are demons, too."

She shook her head. She fell to her knees and whispered, "Angel. He's an Angel. Angel blood is in us."

Jordan growled. He grabbed his dagger and stomped to the door.

"Where are you going?"

He stopped, but kept his back to her, his shoulders tense and square.

"I'm going to find those . . . men . . . you spoke of," he said through clenched teeth. "If they rose from the dead, as you say, I am sure they have answers about *this*." He flicked his hand at Father's abandoned bedding. "And while I'm gone, you can clear your head and accept the truth for what it is."

Cassandra stared wordlessly as her brother disappeared through the door. Now alone, she let the emotions overcome her. She collapsed on her side, curled into herself by the fire and sobbed. She cried for Father, she cried for her brother's obvious delusions and she cried for herself, for being left alone with so many unanswered questions. She cried herself to sleep.

She dreamt of Father in all his Angel glory and she also dreamt of demons. She felt their darkness, their *evil*. She knew, even in her dreams, Father was not a demon. The idea was impossible. How she and Jordan had seen something so different as Father rose from his deathbed, she didn't understand. But she knew in her heart—in her soul—that Father was *good*. And that he had returned to Heaven to be with Mother.

When she awoke, light streamed through the cracks in the grass hut's west walls, indicating late afternoon. She glanced around to see Jordan hadn't returned and her eyes drifted over to Father's empty bedding and then away. She wasn't ready to face it yet. She rose and stepped outside. And blinked.

How could the day still be so bright and beautiful after all that had happened? How could the birds sound so happy and the air smell so sweet when her heart felt heavy and tight in her chest? When loneliness like she'd never felt before weighed her down like a boulder tied to her neck? This world that was exactly the same, yet completely different to her, left her feeling disoriented. She no longer knew what to do with herself. There were chores to be done and food to gather, but everyday life seemed so irrelevant now. So she lay in the grass and stared at the sky, tears seeping down her temples and into her hair.

Thin clouds passed over, shadows grew as the sun fell lower in the west and still she lay there. The tears eventually dried, but she still felt so sad. So empty. So alone. A small voice in the back of her mind told her to get up, to go on with life as Father would want. But she couldn't bring herself to move.

A crashing through the woods startled her to alertness. She shot upright and peered across the clearing. A large shadow moved within the trees, quickly coming closer. She thought of Jordan at first, but this figure was too large and too slow to be him. *The wolf.* Her heart picked up speed. She jumped to her feet. Then the figure emerged from the trees and she blew out a breath. It *was* her brother.

His body looked misshapen, however, and he moved as if weighed down by something heavy. As he came closer, she realized he had a man draped across his shoulders. She ran across the clearing toward them.

"Jordan, what happened?" she demanded as she neared them. Her brother's face was smudged with dirt, but he appeared to be unharmed. The man he held, however, was covered in mud and blood.

"Wolf . . . man," the man said and though it came out as a whisper, she recognized the voice.

"*Niko?*" she asked with disbelief.

His lids slowly lifted, revealing the familiar olive-green eyes. His entire face gnarled with pain but his eyes sparked as he seemed to recognize her. Then Jordan dropped him on the ground with a thud. Niko grunted and passed out.

"Jordan! He's hurt."

"He's probably dead," Jordan said, collapsing to the ground himself.

Cassandra dropped to her knees next to Niko. He still wore the torn chiton from yesterday, his muscular chest and torso exposed. Rather than the one superficial cut he'd had before, rows of long gashes covered his chest now, as if long claws had shredded his skin. Blood and pus gushed from the battle wound in his thigh. She pushed his sweat- and blood-matted hair from his neck and felt for his life signs. A heartbeat pulsed beneath her fingers.

"He's still alive. We must get him inside."

"He won't be for long. Why bother?"

"Jordan!" Cassandra admonished. "How can you be so cruel?"

"*Cruel?* I risked my life for him and he doesn't even have the decency to live long enough to explain."

Her anger flared, but so did curiosity. "Explain what?"

"That wolf. It wasn't normal, Cassandra. Too big and too intelligent. As if it weren't entirely animal."

"The wolf that chased me," Cassandra murmured.

Jordan glared at Niko's unconscious body. "And now we'll know nothing more about it."

"And what makes you think Niko knows anything?"

"He keeps muttering, 'wolf' and 'man.' He's trying to say something but always falls unconscious before anything else comes out."

Cassandra lifted her brows. "Well, he's still alive. Even if you don't have the decency to care for him as a human being, if you want answers, help me get him to the house."

"You really believe you can save him?"

"I don't know for certain, but I definitely can't if we leave him out here. He won't survive the chill of night. And what if that wolf returns?"

Jordan shook his head and then jerked it toward Niko. "He got a good slash at it with his sword just before he collapsed. Then the wolf saw me coming and ran away, probably to its death."

"You didn't make sure? You didn't kill it yourself?"

When Jordan didn't answer, Cassandra cut her eyes toward him. He shook his head, without further explanation. He hid something from her, she could tell, but she had more pressing issues to worry about. She lifted Niko's arm and draped it over her shoulder.

"Well, if you won't help me, I'll do it myself."

She hoped Niko remained unconscious because he would never understand how a woman half his weight could carry him. Jordan rolled his eyes and blew a frustrated grunt through his nose. Then he rose to his feet and lifted Niko's limp body in his own arms.

When they entered the hut, Cassandra's eyes immediately slid to Father's empty bedding. But she just couldn't disturb it. Not now. And not with a filthy, bloody stranger. She gestured to Jordan to lay Niko on her own bedding. With a patient to tend to and her brother nearby, the overwhelming loneliness disappeared. She went to work, cleaning Niko up and caring for his wounds.

Jordan collapsed into his own bedding and fell right to sleep. Cassandra stayed by Niko's side throughout the night, though he remained unconscious the entire time. His skin flamed with fever and she rubbed water over his body to cool it. The herb treatments in his wounds kept turning black, gagging her with a bitter odor and requiring her to change them frequently. As his life signs became stronger, he slept more fitfully, tossing and thrashing, crying out and whispering, "Man-wolf." But by the time the sun rose high in the sky, the herbs no longer turned black in his wounds, his skin no longer burned with intense fever and he settled into a calmer sleep.

Jordan finally awoke, barely glanced at Niko's sleeping form and set out to hunt and gather fruit. He stayed away throughout the morning and into the afternoon. Niko never woke, never even stirred. Cassandra looked longingly at Father's bed as the thought of a nap tugged at her barely coherent mind, but she was afraid to leave Niko's side. His life signs remained weaker than normal and his skin still felt warm, but not as hot as he'd been through the night. She made herself stay awake until Jordan could relieve her. Surely he had enough compassion to keep an eye on the sick and injured man long enough for her to get a little rest. But when he returned, he had no interest in staying for long.

After they ate a meal of rabbit and berries, he asked her to go outside with him. Cassandra looked at Niko's sleeping form and sighed. She didn't want to leave him in case he woke, but anything she and Jordan had to discuss—their father, their belongings, their future—this stranger didn't need to hear. She followed Jordan out the door and far into the clearing, which was turning gray in the fading light of dusk.

"We need to leave in the morning," Jordan said as he turned around to face her.

She blinked at him. "Leave? Why?"

He'd just brought home a month's worth of supplies. They would only need fresh food, easily found in the nearby woods and streams. Why did they need to go already? And did he actually plan to take her with him? This caught her by surprise, but the thought of leaving crushed her heart. This was the last place Father had been. The last place she'd ever feel his presence.

"I'm not leaving," she said before Jordan could even explain his reasoning. "Not yet."

"Don't you want answers?"

"Answers to what?"

"To what Father revealed to us. He kept it hidden all these years, so there must be a reason he told us. Don't you want to know what that reason is? Don't you want to know more about us?"

"And just where do you plan on finding these answers?"

Jordan's eyes lit up. "There are others out there like us. I know where to find them."

Cassandra's eyes narrowed. "What are you talking about? You know others like us? How?"

"I don't exactly *know* them, but four of them live in a village about a five-days' walk from here. I've been there many times over the years and they don't look a day older than the first time I saw them. We have aged faster than them."

"Impossible."

"I've seen it myself."

She put her fists on her hips. "Then how could they live in the village all these years and no one has questioned them?"

"They only come outside at night and the rest of the village ignores them, as if they don't even see them. Besides, only *I* have lived long enough to notice."

"So they live secret lives while everyone else sleeps? Others ignore them, as if they aren't even real people? If all this is true and they're older than us but look younger, well . . . they sound like . . . like demons, Jordan."

"Exactly."

Cassandra's eyes widened. "And you want to seek them out? Have you lost your mind?"

"We're no different! We don't sneak around at night, but instead hide out on the edge of civilization. Why would Father make us live like this? Because he was afraid people would know what we really are."

"But we're *not* demons. We're from ang—"

Jordan cut her off with a roar. "Don't even say it. Stop lying to yourself!"

She narrowed her eyes, raised up on her toes to lean toward him and lifted her chin. She kept her voice low and her words deliberate. "I am *not* evil. I am *not* a demon. And I am *not* going with you."

Then she turned on her heel and stalked off toward the hut. Jordan's hand clamped down on her shoulder and he spun her around.

"At least come with me to get answers. They *must* know something."

"You can get your answers. I don't need them. I know who and what I am. It changes nothing. I don't care about the rest."

"I can't just leave you here alone!"

She threw her arms in the air. "Why not? Isn't that what you always wanted? Your freedom to do as you please without worrying about your father and sister? I can take care of myself. Now, I have a sick man to tend to and I won't leave him to die, either." She turned again and stomped toward the hut.

"Is that what it is?" Jordan asked, catching up with her. "This strange man? You'll stay for him rather than go with your own brother?"

"I stay for myself, but, yes, I will take care of him until he is well."

"I want him gone. He leaves immediately."

"Leave?" She let out a bark of a laugh. "You know he's too ill. I thought you had questions for him anyway."

"I won't wait around for answers he probably doesn't have. I already know where to find them. And I will not have him here with you alone."

"Then don't leave. You're the one insisting on going."

Jordan stopped. "So that's it? You're choosing a stranger over me? Over your own family, all that you have left?"

Cassandra didn't answer, didn't even acknowledge the question. Her decision had nothing to do with Niko. Well, little to do with him. She wasn't ready to go yet, to leave Father's memories behind. She needed peace to grieve and time to figure out what to do with the rest of her life. If Jordan wanted to be a part of it, she would be happy. And if he insisted on leaving, she would accept that, too. But she would not go with him now.

"You can't do enough good in the world to cleanse the blood in your veins," Jordan yelled. "You're a demon. Father was a liar and a coward but now you know the truth!"

Cassandra stopped cold. Her heart pounded in her chest. Her nostrils flared and her eyes sparked. She spun around and strode several paces toward the man she called her brother. Jordan stood with his arms crossed over his chest, his muscles bulging out of his chiton, his face twisted.

"How *dare* you?" she demanded, her voice rising several octaves. "How dare you speak of Father like that?"

"Face the truth, little sister. He lied to us. And you—" He jabbed a finger at her chest. "—you want that man. You want to lie naked in his bed. Admit it."

Cassandra's face burned and her eyes bulged as she stared at her brother. She wanted to deny his accusations, but anger kept any words from forming. Her silence seemed to only fuel Jordan's anger.

"See?" he sneered. "Demon blood. It makes you want him. It makes you choose a stranger over me, makes you want to behave like a prostitute. If you deny it, you're a liar just like Father."

"Do not speak of him that way!" Cassandra yelled. "Do not speak of him at all."

"Demon blood makes us act like this, little sister. That's why I am the way I am. And you are no different. Not really. I see it in your eyes. Your lust. Your desire. Your defiance. Thank Father for all that." He leaned back and stroked his chin. "Oh, but you can't. He conveniently *died* instead of facing his own children. The coward I always thought he was!"

Sickened by Jordan's words, Cassandra could think of only one way to shut him up. She pulled her hand back and let it fly forward. But she didn't slap him. She curled her hand into a fist and punched him in the jaw. As strong as he was, he staggered several steps backward. His blue eyes widened with surprise and his hand went to his injured face. Cassandra turned once again and never looked back.

When she entered the hut, she was grateful to find Niko still sleeping soundly. She sank to her knees and cried. Life had already changed so much. *Why did Father wait until he died to tell us? Is Jordan right?* She refused to believe her brother's theory. But she also couldn't explain his behavior. *How could he be so cruel? So selfish? What happened to him?* They were so different and she almost had to wonder if he did have demon blood in him.

But if he did . . .

"Is everything okay?" a husky voice asked.

Cassandra looked up in surprise to find Niko watching her from his bed—*her* bed—with those strangely beautiful green eyes. She scrubbed the tears from her face.

"Not really," she admitted, but then she lifted her chin and went to him. She held her hand to his cheek and found his skin temperature to be nearly normal. "How are you?"

"I think I'll be okay." Niko covered her hand with his, pressing it tighter against his face. "With you here."

He closed his eyes and drifted off again. Her hand on his face suddenly felt more intimate than the touch of a healer. She should pull away, but she liked the feeling of his large hand over her small one. She liked the strange tingle of his skin against hers. She couldn't help but wonder what it would feel like to have all of him pressed against all of her. Then she gasped and yanked her hand away.

She sprang back, landing on her feet near Father's bed. *How could I think such a thing? Is the demon blood coming out in me?* She looked at her palm that had pressed against Niko's face. She'd never felt anything like that. It felt *good*, not bad. But Mother had told her many things that felt good weren't. Especially when it came to men. And punching Jordan had also felt good . . . at the time. Now her heart squeezed with guilt for hurting her own brother.

She didn't know what to believe. Was she letting Jordan get to her? Or did she just prove him right? But how could she be a demon? She cared for people. Healed strangers. Gave them everything she could. But what Jordan said . . . what just happened . . . *Lust and desire*—Jordan said he'd seen it in her eyes. Was that what she'd just felt? Was wanting to be close to a man wrong?

Cassandra looked at her Father's empty bedding. She bent down and smelled him in the blankets.

"I miss you, Father," she cried. "I miss you so much. I need you. I *do* need to know."

She pulled the blankets back, wanting to crawl underneath them, to close her eyes and not think about angels and demons anymore. The thought of being a demon—even half a demon—scared her so much, yet she thought it might be something she would have to face. Maybe her vision had been clouded and confused when Father rose to leave them. Maybe that hadn't been him at all, with the glorious white wings, looking like an Angel. Maybe Jordan had seen the truth, while she had seen only what she wanted . . . what she wanted to believe.

She looked over her shoulder at the door, wondering if Jordan had already left, if it was too late to catch him. But she was too exhausted to even try. She would decide in the morning if she really wanted the answers he sought.

She slid into Father's bedding and began to lay her head down when something pricked her shoulder. She reached underneath herself, pulled out what felt like a twig and held it up to the fire—a small feather, about the length of her thumb. It seemed to almost glow, it shone so white, with gold at the tip of its quill. She held it to her nose and smelled Father. She brushed the feathery softness against her lips as she lay down. She smiled and closed her eyes.

And she saw Father, hovering above her, just like his last moments with them. When he rose with white wings outspread. When he looked so inhumanly magnificent. When he looked like his real self: an Angel.

No, she didn't need answers from anyone else. She had to believe in herself, in her own eyes, in her own heart. As she'd told Jordan, what they now knew didn't change anything. She would still care for others and heal them when possible. Her heart still desperately wanted that kind of love Father and Mother shared. And how could a demon want to care for others? Want love?

Jordan is wrong. She must find him and convince him before he ruined his life.

Chapter 4

Jordan rubbed his jaw as he watched his sister disappear into the raggedy grass hut they called a home. He'd taught her how to throw that punch, never expecting she'd use it on him. If the forming bruise didn't pulse on his skin and into his bone right now, he'd never believe her capable of physically harming another person. She had the strength and ability, but not the temperament. He wasn't surprised to find that perfect Cassandra wasn't so perfect after all, though. He'd suspected she had a streak buried deeply under all that goodness and now he knew how to pull it out of her.

He turned his back to their home and pulled his dagger out of his belt, swiping it at the thigh-high grass as he walked to the far edge of the clearing. His anger, ignited by Father's death and fueled by Cassandra's rejection, cooled as new plans formed in his mind. Perhaps Father's death—an inexact term for someone who'd revealed their true dark self and then just disappeared, but the only way Jordan could describe it—hadn't ruined everything after all. He just needed to convince Cassandra of their potential and how much better their lives could be. She should be easier to convince than Father, who had been so cowardly and stubborn.

Jordan's plans had begun forming over a decade ago, although the idea had planted itself in his mind many, many years before then, while Mother was still alive. Once he had become a man, he'd grown restless, knowing there was more to experience in this world than their secluded lives. Although the rest of his family seemed happy, he was not. He wanted more. So Father took him along on supply trips and taught him how to barter in the marketplace, hunt in the wilderness and fight with a sword and dagger. While at the market one day, a rival army attacked the town. Jordan and Father had to fight or be taken as slaves, leaving Mother and Cassandra on their own. Jordan saw clearly that he and Father were superior warriors compared to any of the trained soldiers on either side.

After experiencing the thrill of victory, he questioned Father on the way home, asking why they didn't just overthrow the rulers of a small village, claim their spot as leaders and create a real home for their family. Father quickly dismissed Jordan's notions, explaining that although civilization was a threat to them because of their differences, they were to treat people with kindness, respect and love.

"It is not our place to rule a village," Father had said. "We're to serve the people however we can, but never abuse the abilities we've been given."

Serve the people who would lock them up or stone them to death? Jordan didn't understand and eventually decided Father was simply a coward.

After Mother died, Father and Cassandra found solace in each other, tightening their bond, while Jordan drifted further away. He began making the supply trips on his own since Father didn't want to leave Cassandra alone. Jordan became braver and more assertive while in the villages, no longer willing to blend in and hide. He came to understand people better, becoming more involved with them, and he realized Father had lied. He'd kept them away from the villages for no good reason at all—they could have easily assimilated and settled down. Father's unwarranted fear had forced them to live as barbarians. The realization that his father was not only a coward but also a liar brought darkness into Jordan's heart.

He tried to accomplish what Father hadn't allowed for them—a place in a village where they would be accepted, where he could join the army and eventually prove that he wasn't just as good as everyone else, but even better. They gave him the attention he desired and he soaked it all in, especially the praise from the powerful. But eventually they'd always rejected him. They didn't trust his loyalty because he had no "home," no tribe or city-state he belonged to. When they asked who his father was and he couldn't give an answer they knew, they insulted him and his family. Once he realized he'd never be truly accepted, the darkness in his heart grew.

One day, he vowed, he would rule all of them. Just as he'd told Father years before, he'd take over a small village and grow his empire from there. He'd get his revenge on all those kings and lords who'd rejected him. But he'd needed Father's help and now Father was gone.

He still had Cassandra, though, and she'd just shown promise of what she could be, if he could convince her. And this revelation from Father—demon blood in their veins! He'd been shocked and angry at first, but the more he'd thought about it over the last two days, the more it made sense. He'd obviously felt it more strongly than the rest of his family, explaining the darkness in him they didn't have—or, rather, that they suppressed. Now he understood and this was better than anything he could have ever hoped for. But before he could do anything, especially convince his sister of the truth, he needed more information.

He sheathed his dagger and broke into a run.

He ran through the night . . . and the following day . . . and that night. If they had walked the journey, laden with supplies and belongings, it would have taken them five days to reach the village where he knew those others lived. But nothing weighed Jordan down now and the possibilities of a new and better life fed his desire to get there sooner rather than later. He stopped to rest only once and approached the outskirts of the village on the second afternoon.

Knowing the others slept during the day and left their home only at night, he stopped by a pond outside of town. Pausing just long enough to untie his sandals and leave them on the bank, he strode straight into the water until it reached his waist. He dove under the surface, relishing the coolness and washing the dirt and sweat from his skin. Then he removed his chiton, cleaned it as best as he could, and threw it at a tree on the bank, where it caught perfectly on a branch to dry. He untied the leather strap holding his blond hair and tossed it to the bank, as well.

Free from cumbersome clothing and restraints, he swam several laps across the pond and then floated on his back. When he was relaxed enough to catch a nap, he stood and turned toward the bank. To find himself not alone.

She sat about twenty strides away, her legs curled underneath her, her black hair hanging loosely over her shoulders and down her back. Her golden skin was the color of field workers', but her blue peplos and the jewels adorning her neck, arms and fingers revealed that she came from money. She didn't belong here, but in her home or palace, tucked away in her gynaeceum. No man accompanied her now, not even a slave, which meant ... what? Jordan could think of only one reason. *This will be fun.* Her large, dark eyes—darker than Cassandra's—didn't stop staring at him, even as he emerged from the water, exposing his full nudity.

He wasn't surprised by this. He had the hard body of a warrior and even the most virtuous couldn't bring themselves to turn away. More than one woman had told him his body was as glorious as the gods'. He hadn't had to pay a hetaera in years—they wanted to pay *him* just for the thrill of running their hands over his body.

Long ago he'd lost interest in relationships with women. They were all heart-crushing and greedy liars, promising themselves to one man while running off with another who was richer and more powerful. But he hadn't lost interest in sex and if they wanted to pay him for it, all the better. Although this beauty could obviously afford it, he would probably let her enjoy him for free.

"You don't have to just look," he said as he stood on the bank. "I do allow a touch and a taste of the goods before buying."

She stood and he had to concentrate to keep his friend between his legs down. She had the body of a goddess. He'd never seen a peplos fall so perfectly over full breasts and hips, stating so much while revealing little. She lifted an eyebrow as her eyes traveled down and back up his own body. A smile played on her luscious lips.

"Too bad for you that I have no need for another slave," she said, her husky voice sending a thrill down his spine. He reached for his chiton and bunched it front of himself, not out of modesty, but to cover his growing friend, betraying his interest. Such desire was not helpful for bargaining.

"I'm not a slave," he said. "I'm a performer. I can entertain you like no other."

She studied his face, her hand caressing her neck as she seemed to consider his offer.

"Again, too bad for you," she finally said. "I don't need an entertainer either."

She turned and sauntered off toward town, her peplos swishing against her legs and her hips teasing him even more.

"Then what *do* you need?" The words spewed out of his mouth before he could stop them.

"A lover who can give me more than a five-minute thrill," she said over her shoulder.

His chiton fell from his hand, exposing his large, hard friend. *Traitor*, he thought at it. It throbbed as he watched her leave.

"She's just a hetaera anyway," he muttered.

She flicked her hand in a strange wave and flames exploded at his feet, licking at his calves. He yelped and jumped back into the water. The cold water, at least, doused his desire.

☙

Jordan slept a few hours until dusk, then ran for the village. He'd been watching these men for several years, since realizing they were more like himself and his family than everyone else, but he'd never been able to follow them when they left their home at night—they moved even faster than he did. He didn't want to take the chance of missing them tonight, so he hurried to be outside their door when darkness fell. He arrived just in time to hear them stirring inside the home they shared. The door opened before he had a chance to announce himself, and a tall, pale man with dark hair and black eyes peered out at him.

"Are you lost?" he asked.

Jordan swallowed down his sudden fear, a rare feeling for him. "No. I have come here for you."

The man lifted an eyebrow. "For me? You are mistaken. No—"

"I know what you are," Jordan interrupted. "And I am like you. You can tell me what no one else can."

The man threw back his head and laughed, an eerie sound that sent a chill up Jordan's spine. Another man, also white-skinned and dark-haired, approached behind the first, as if drawn by the strange laughter.

"Vlasis," the laughing man said, "this youth thinks he's like us!"

The other man made a dismissive sound and waved his hand, then turned and left. The first abruptly stopped and peered at Jordan with narrowed eyes that changed from midnight-black to a glowing red. He leaned forward.

"You are *nothing* like us."

Jordan stood his ground, ignoring the growing and inexplicable fear. "You don't age. You're strong and move faster than the eye can see. You call me a youth but most men my age are stooped and wrinkled. I can out-lift, out-throw and out-run any human."

"But can you do this?" His lips lifted in a snarl, exposing fangs like an animal's, just like those men who'd been chasing Cassandra. His eyes glowed even brighter. Jordan couldn't stop himself from taking a step back. "Do you live for the hunt? For the taste of human blood? Do you excite at their fear? I think not. You are *not* like us, the immortal ones."

Jordan lifted his chin, still fighting the terror that tried to wind its tendrils around him. "I may not be exactly like you, but I am close. Unlike you, I am only *half*-demon."

The man drew back slightly and seemed to consider Jordan for a long moment.

"Demon?" he asked. "You believe you are half-demon?"

"I don't believe. I *know*. My father was Andrew, a fallen angel. Surely you know of him."

The man peered at him again, seeming to almost show an interest. Then his nostrils flared and he sniffed the air with the arrogance of a king.

"No matter. You are still nothing like us. We are not demons. We are *predators*. The most dangerous predators on this Earth." He leaned toward Jordan again, exposing those dagger-like teeth. His voice came out in a feral snarl. "Now be gone. Before you become my prey."

Moving too fast to see, the man disappeared and the door slammed in Jordan's face. He stood motionless, his mouth hanging open. *How dare he!* He took a step forward and lifted his fist for the wooden door.

"I wouldn't," came a husky yet feminine voice from the shadow of the next house.

Jordan spun, his dagger out and ready. She chuckled and a figure emerged halfway out of the darkness—the same woman from the pond earlier, once again out when she shouldn't be. She wiggled her fingers for him to follow as she sauntered down the path leading to the village center. His eyes cut to the door and then back to her, and he was torn by his need for answers and his desire to know this raven-haired beauty.

"I can help you." Her whispered words floated to him, although she was too far away for him to possibly hear. "I know who you are and I know who you need to meet. I can take you."

Jordan hesitated. He half-turned toward the door and renewed fear washed over him. He hurried after the woman.

He followed her out of town to a surprisingly small home on the outskirts of the village. She led him inside, where piles of pillows and blankets surrounded a low wooden table and a fire crackled in the stone hearth. A black pot sat in the coals, a sweet yet strange smelling steam swirling from its boiling contents. He looked around, but it appeared as though no one else was there.

"Whose home is this?" Jordan didn't think it could be hers. She looked as though she should live in a palace or, at least, in a stone-walled, two-story home with a courtyard, kitchen and andron. But, then again, she apparently wasn't like other women, controlled by men. Which both thrilled and bothered Jordan.

"Mine." She sank into one of the oversized pillows.

"Where are all your slaves?"

The woman smiled and her eyes sparkled, as if she knew a secret. In fact, Jordan thought, she always seemed to look as though she knew something he didn't.

"They are all around me," she said, waving her hand in the air, although the one-room house was apparently empty. "*Any*one can be my slave if I so desire."

Jordan took a step backward toward the door. "I said I am not one."

She laughed. "And I said I don't need one. Not right now. And not you."

"Then what do you want with me?" If she wanted a night together, paid or not, he knew he'd succumb. There was something about her that made him ache with desire.

"It's not what *I* want with *you*. It's what you want from me. What you need from me."

He lifted an eyebrow. "I need nothing. However . . ." He took a step toward her and pulled the strap from his hair, letting it fall loose against his shoulders. ". . . I do want—"

She laughed, cutting him off. "Oh, I know what you *want*. It's quite tempting. But not now, Jordan."

His eyes narrowed. "How do you know my name?"

"I've been waiting for you. I've been sent for you. I have the answers you seek."

He didn't say anything, only stood in the middle of her pillow-laden, fire-lit room, and stared at her with bewilderment. She pointed to a plush pillow.

"Sit and I will explain."

He hesitated. "Are *you* a demon?"

"No. I am Eris."

"What is an Eris?"

She rolled her eyes. "That is my name. Sit, Jordan. Be comfortable. Here, have some wine."

Eris held out a cup that appeared from nowhere. He took it and sniffed its aroma, then lifted it to his lips for a small taste. The woman was too mysterious to trust. He decided the wine was safe, however, and took a deeper draw, then sat on the pillow she indicated.

"Do you know those men?" he asked. "How do you know me? And what do you mean that you were sent for me?"

"Those were not *men*. Those were vampyres. They are not like you at all. You are still alive. They are not. Not quite."

Jordan peered suspiciously at the wine, wondering if she had indeed poisoned him.

"Explain or I leave."

"You came looking for demons. I will take you to the true demons. The Ancients. They sent me for you, knowing you would come looking. Those vampyres are their pets. You want nothing to do with them. Trust me."

"Why should I?"

She gave him that coy smile again. "Because you want to. Because you have to. If you want the answers you seek."

"But you are *not* a demon? Are you a vampyre?"

An angry hiss escaped her lips. "Certainly not! They survive off *blood*. Created by the Ancients for the sole purpose of preying on humans. They pretend as though they are civilized but they are more beastly than any natural animal on this Earth."

"Who are the Ancients?"

"The Ancients are of the original demons. The fallen angels you seek." She lifted an eyebrow, questioning if he understood. He nodded. "They are the origins of the Daemoni, demons who Satan ordered to create an army on Earth. They have created many kinds of creatures and beasts, including their beloved vampyres."

"And if you are not a vampyre . . . ?"

She smiled coyly again. "My father was a sorcerer—a demon who possessed a human, allowing him to roam the Earth while keeping his magick. My mother was human. Her blood diluted his powers, but I still have the magick of our strongest warlocks. However, warlocks prefer the physical fight and I prefer to fight with my mind." She waved her hand over her enticing body. "Why would I risk harming this?"

"Why indeed?" Jordan asked, momentarily distracted. He took another swallow of wine, trying to focus on her meaning. "You have powerful magick? Did you start that fire under my feet today?"

She leaned forward on her forearms, her golden breasts pushing out over the top of her peplos. Her voice came out even lower than usual. "I am *not* a prostitute. I couldn't let you get away with calling me one."

Jordan licked his lips and forced himself to pull his eyes away from her luscious curves. He looked up at her face unabashedly. Anyone else would have feared her and what she'd just told him about magick and demons, but, of course, he was not like most people. Knowing she had demon blood, just like him, made her even more desirable to him. He could tell she wanted him, too. He reached toward her face. She grabbed his wrist and pushed his hand back at him.

"I said, not now. Whether you believe it or not, I am not that kind of woman."

Jordan doubted that. He also doubted she could so easily deny her desire for him. Something else had kept her from undressing them both the minute they entered the house. Because she was that kind of woman. He took another swig of wine, emptying his cup. She flicked her finger and it was suddenly full again. He looked up at her.

"You're not a sorcerer or a warlock, so what are you?" he asked.

"Despite my power, they call me a mere witch." She shrugged. "What they call me matters not. All that matters is my power. Something for you to keep in mind."

"Are you part of this army of Satan then?"

"I am Daemoni, yes."

"How do I become Daemoni?"

She studied his face for a long moment. "You want to fight for Satan?"

"Demon blood runs through my veins. And so does that of a warrior. Why wouldn't I?"

She made a sniffing sound, similar to the one the vampyre had made earlier, as though dismissing him. "We shall see if you have the heart for it. The Ancients will know and they want to meet you."

"They want to meet me? They know of me?" He paused. "But of course they do. My father was one of them, after all. And so am I. Partially, at least."

"They've been waiting for you for centuries, before you were even born. Ever since the prophecy about your mother."

"What prophecy?"

"It's not my place to say. The Ancients will tell you, if they so desire. If you want to still meet them."

"Of course I do."

Eris looked at him thoughtfully. "You seem so eager for this. But what about your sister? What about human life? Do you treasure anything besides yourself?"

"I care for my sister, but she is ignorant. One reason I seek the demons is to prove to her that we belong with them. We are *not* human. We are *better*."

Eris smiled again and nodded. "Perfect."

ᴄ⁊

When Jordan awoke the next morning, he at first believed he had dreamt the night before, until he realized he lay on one of Eris's pillows. Then he thought he must have drunk too much wine, because the conversation felt so unreal in the morning's light. He had no doubts, however, about the demons. He probably shouldn't have trusted Eris so wholeheartedly, but he felt she was the only way to find these Ancients . . . to find the answers he sought.

"You do not hide in the darkness of night," he said pointedly as she prepared her house for their departure. "Not like those . . . others."

He still wasn't sure about the reality of that part of the conversation—men who drank blood.

"The vampyres?" she asked, confirming that they had, indeed, talked about them. "They prefer the night, when people are more frightened. They feed off their fear nearly as much as they feed off their blood. The sun also tends to weaken them. But not me. Not any mage."

"Mage?"

"Those of us with magick powers. The vampyres have a different kind of magick, given to them by the Ancients when they created the first one. They can boost their power by feeding off a mage, but that would be very stupid of them."

"It sounds quite wise of them to me, if it increases their power."

Eris growled. "Vampyres kill their food more often than not and the Ancients don't want the mages' numbers to dwindle. We are precious, too. Come. We must leave. We have a long trip ahead of us."

Jordan's brows furrowed. "Where are we going?"

"North. As far North as we can possibly go."

Chapter 5

Cassandra sat on the grass in front of the hut, her knees drawn to her chest and her arms wrapped around them. And she watched. Just as she'd been doing all day. Waiting for Jordan's return. She thought he would have come in last night after walking off his anger. She couldn't believe he would just leave her alone, especially so soon after losing Father.

Her stomach clenched, nearly making her retch, every time she thought of her fist hitting his jaw. She couldn't believe now that she'd actually punched him—she'd never lost control like that in her life. Jordan was the short-tempered one. Not her. And maybe if she hadn't gone so far, he would have come home by now. As the sun dipped below the treetops in the distance, casting long shadows into the clearing, she sighed and finally rose to her feet.

The few times she'd checked on Niko, he'd been sleeping soundly. His fever had broken and his wounds no longer leaked pus or that strange black ooze. He'd probably be in bed at least another day. When she slipped inside now, though, his eyes were wide open. His lips turned upward into a tired smile.

"My angel," he said.

Cassandra stopped and her hand flew to her throat. "What did you say?"

"I've heard stories from the Jews about angels," he said, his voice low but steady. "I never believed them before, but now . . . perhaps this is what they meant. Perhaps they saw someone like you and thought she was from the heavens . . . so beautiful and radiant . . . and kind."

Cassandra blushed and dropped her hand to her side, her heart settling once she realized he didn't know something he shouldn't. Father had told her about the Jews—the people who had run him and Mother out of town once, threatening to kill them. They'd seen Mother's unusual strength, which apparently she gained when he shared his blood with her. Father had never taken them so far east again and never allowed Mother—or Cassandra, once she was born—in a village again.

She went over to her line of clay pots that held her herbs and began mixing Niko's medicine.

"So you believe in angels?" she asked.

He chuckled. "About as much as I believe in one god who has created and is master of everything."

Cassandra turned to look at him. "And you *don't* believe that?"

"Of course not. There are many gods. Zeus, Mars, Apollo, Adonis. And we can't forget the goddesses."

She remembered Jordan's stories now, of people who didn't share Father's beliefs. Her beliefs. "I believe in only God, the one Almighty God. That is what Mother and Father taught me."

Niko chuckled again. "How can there be only one god? How can one single person be master of the entire world and the stars and the heavens and Hades?"

"Because He is not a person. He is God." Her firm tone

kept Niko from arguing. She poured water into the bowl of herbs and set it near the fire to steep.

"Well, if his angels are as beautiful as you, I could be convinced to believe," he finally said.

Her face heated again. *If he only knew.* But she could never tell him, never tell anyone. Because everyone else would believe as Jordan did—that they had demon blood, not angel.

Caring for Niko's wounds provided the distraction she needed from worrying about Jordan. In fact, he made her completely forget everything for a while. Now that he was awake and lucid, talking to her and taking everything in, she once again became more aware of him as a man—a very attractive man—rather than a patient. Her hands trembled by the time she finished with him and she had to sit on the other side of the fire, as far away from him as possible, to settle her nerves.

"You were quite upset last night," Niko said. "At least, I *think* it was last night."

He'd heard her crying? What else had he heard? She thought he'd been sleeping the whole time.

"I hope I haven't caused problems with you and . . ." He looked at her questioningly.

"My brother, Jordan. He brought you here." Cassandra blinked back tears and stared at the fire. Apparently Niko hadn't heard everything and she would never tell him the horrible things Jordan had said. She wouldn't make him sound like a monster. After all, he'd saved Niko's life. She shook her head. "He's just upset. Our father—" Her breath hitched. "He died the other day."

There. She said it. Aloud. Although she had seen him as an Angel, understood he hadn't died like other people did, like Mother had, it really was the proper explanation. He was no longer here, on Earth with them. He was in Heaven with Mother now. For all intents and purposes, he was dead. The tears spilled. She missed him so much.

Niko moved to get up, but she held her hand out and shook her head.

"I'm okay," she said. "You need to stay in bed."

She wiped the tears from her face and they sat in silence for a long time, both staring at the fire.

"My father died many years ago, when I was a child," Niko finally said.

Cassandra looked at him, her heart squeezing for him, although it had been so long ago and her own pain was so fresh.

"I'm sorry," she said.

"He never saw me become a soldier. He'd always told me I'd be a strong warrior . . ." His voice trailed off as he seemed to lose himself in the past.

"You still have other family?" Cassandra asked, hoping the thought would cheer him. She was rewarded with a heart-stopping smile and he told her all about his mother and sisters, his nieces and nephews. His special fondness for the children came clear in his voice.

"And you?"

Cassandra shook her head. "Only Jordan. He's my twin brother."

"Your mother?"

"She died many years ago. It's only been Father, Jordan and me. And now . . ."

"Just you and Jordan," Niko finished for her. But she didn't know if she could even believe that. She felt as though it might just be herself now. She shook her head.

"I don't know," she whispered. "I don't know if he'll come back."

"Of course he'll come back. He wouldn't leave you here alone. Would he? What kind of brother would do that?"

Cassandra wanted to defend Jordan, to say he was a good brother and would return to take care of her, but it would be too close to a lie. She lifted her chin.

"He has his own life to live, as do I. I don't need him to

take care of me."

Niko eyed her for a moment, then lay down. He didn't say all women needed a man to take care of them, as she'd expected, as Jordan had always told her. Was he different than Jordan, having grown up with a mother who'd raised her children on her own? Or was he just too ill to argue with her?

Cassandra knew she could take care of herself. She didn't worry about that part of being alone. Her heart hurt from Jordan's absence because he was all she had. They shared a long life of memories and now he was the only person in the whole world with whom she had any ties. Where was he?

❡

The days and nights passed. Niko grew stronger. Jordan never came back.

Niko would soon be ready to return home and the thought of his leaving bothered Cassandra more each time she considered it. She enjoyed his company and although her belly still quivered whenever he looked at her with those olive-green eyes, she became accustomed to it. In fact, she liked these new feelings he gave her. Though they'd known each other for only a few days, she knew him better than she'd ever known anyone outside of her own family. She would miss him terribly. In fact, her chest already tightened with longing when he went off simply to collect firewood or water, and her heart skipped with pleasure when he returned.

Then the days turned into weeks and the weather began to change, bringing a chill to the air and making the nights longer. Niko should have been physically able to leave a long time ago, but every few days, he would seem to lose some of his strength and Cassandra wondered what that wolf had done to him. But by the next morning, he'd be better. Soon, they would both have to leave. Supplies were dwindling.

Normally, Jordan would have returned by now. Even if he'd taken off out of anger, he would have known to bring back supplies. He was gone for good. Cassandra knew this in her heart. Niko would leave her and she would need to face the agora, the marketplace, for the first time ever.

"You should come home with me," Niko said one evening as they ate fish he had caught and a chunk of bread made with the last of the grain and olive oil.

"I can't do that," Cassandra said, shaking her head.

"You know he's not coming back."

She didn't answer him. Admitting it to herself was one thing. Admitting it to Niko made it more real. Anger suddenly overwhelmed her. *How could my own brother do this to me? How could he put me in this position?* She was tired of defending him. She hurled her piece of bread at the ground and sprang to her feet.

"Of course I know that," she shouted, throwing her hands about. "He's arrogant and selfish and cares about no one except himself! He's waited for this time for . . . for*ever*. For the time when he could be free of any obligations. He's out there on his adventures, exploring land and sea. He's probably already forgotten he even has a sister. Yes. I know he's not coming back."

Cassandra stomped outside into the chilly night. She sucked in a deep breath of humid air tainted with the smoky smell from their fire inside. She also smelled the change in seasons as colder weather approached. She threw her head back and blew out the air in a huff of exasperation. The stars above seemed brighter and more numerous than usual and the sky itself felt so close, she thought she could reach up and touch it. She couldn't help but wonder if Jordan stared at the same stars and moon and the thought gave her the sudden urge to lift her hand up and brush away the sparkles as though they were granules of dirt on her tunic. But then that would wipe away possibly the only connection she had with anyone on this Earth.

She hadn't heard Niko follow her out, so she startled at his touch when he placed his hands on her shoulders.

"So why do you care if he returns?" he asked quietly.

Cassandra sighed, ignoring the sting behind her eyes. "Because he's all I have."

Niko stepped around her, facing her. She fell against him and cried into his chest for several minutes. He wrapped his arms around her and held her. When she finally stopped, he lifted his hand and stroked a brush of heat across her cheek, wiping away the tears. Then he placed his finger under her chin and lifted her face toward his.

"You have me," he murmured. His lovely green eyes stared into hers, questioning if she understood. Her heart hammered. Her knees went weak. Too flustered to do anything, she just stood there as he bent over and brushed his lips against hers. A jolt of pleasure charged through her lips and spread through her chest and to her heart. "If you'll have me, that is."

Oh, did she want him. In many more ways than she could comprehend. But it was impossible. She couldn't have a lasting relationship with anyone, no matter how badly she wanted it. Niko may care for her now, but when he found out about her— which he would eventually—he'd probably be part of the crowd that stoned her to death to get rid of the demon. With this thought, she understood Jordan's need to find others like them. She didn't change her mind about what kind of blood coursed through her veins, but she did see how the only people they could ever be around were others like them. And not like Niko.

She swallowed the lump that had formed in her throat. She looked Niko in the eye and, pushing her true feelings into a corner of her heart, she said, "I'm sorry . . . ."

"Please reconsider. The world is very harsh for women. I can protect you."

"I don't need protection."

"But you do. As soon as you set foot in an agora—"

Cassandra's nostrils flared. So Niko was, after all, very much like Jordan in this regard. "Jordan has told me it's no place for a woman. But I'll do what I have to do."

"You don't understand. You go anywhere in any village, they'll see you as a slave. When they realize you have no husband or master, they'll capture you and make you their property. But if you come with me—"

"I can be *your* property?"

Perhaps her accusation wasn't fair, but what Niko told her scared her. When Mother met Father, she'd been fleeing men who'd wanted to take her as a slave after her parents died. Father had saved her from that life. But Cassandra didn't want to go with Niko out of fear . . . or pity. The way he looked at her now reminded her of the way Father used to look at Mother, but, regardless of how parallel their situations seemed to be, she and Niko could never have what they had.

"No, thank you." She turned her back to him, biting her lip to hold back the tears.

"Cassandra, I—"

She spun on him and made her voice come out as hard as possible. "I said no. I can't. I'm sorry."

Niko's eyes turned a stormy gray for a moment as pain filled them. Then he blinked, raised his chin and nodded. "Okay, then. I will not bother you anymore."

He turned back for the hut and went inside without another word. Cassandra hugged herself, not just against the damp, chilly air, but against the coldness she felt inside. She could feel his hurt feelings as if they were her own and she had caused it. She had broken his heart and hers. But she had no choice.

Chapter 6

Jordan and Eris traveled north for weeks. The initial stab of guilt Jordan felt for leaving Cassandra had dissipated into just a twinge and then disappeared altogether as he became more enthralled with everything Eris told him. Eventually, he'd return to his sister, but not until he understood it all and felt sure he could convince her to see things his way. That would take time, especially with this journey taking so long. Eris' patience grew thin with his "human inadequacies."

"I can run faster than any human, including you," he growled, tired of her whining.

"But you cannot flash."

"What do you mean, flash?"

"This." She was instantly gone from his side, standing at the crest of the mountain they climbed. Then just as quickly, she stood next to him again. Jordan was impressed.

"Why can't I?"

"You don't have the power. The Ancients can give it to you. If they want to."

Jordan suggested she flash to keep up with him and they tried the idea, but it was still too slow for Eris. In one flash she could travel farther then he could run in a day. The next morning he awoke to her crouched over a black metal pot sitting in their campfire, waving her hands through the orange steam rising above it. She scooped a bowl into the pot and handed him the foul smelling soup.

"Drink this," she commanded.

Jordan wrinkled his nose. "You can't be serious."

"If you want to travel with me, you need the magick within. We are taking too long and if we don't arrive soon, the Ancients will be angry. You don't want to see them angry."

Jordan drank the soup that tasted as bad as it smelled, struggling to keep it from coming back up. When they were ready, she took his hand and the air whooshed out of his lungs and his vision went black. He stumbled over his own feet when they reappeared. Then she did it again. And again. And again. Each time they appeared somewhere new and, disoriented, he staggered and once even fell, nearly toppling over the edge of a cliff.

"We'll stay here for the night," Eris finally said when they appeared outside a cave on the side of a mountain. She had to shout over the sound of a raging waterfall across the valley. The air here was much colder and crisper than where they had been just that morning—according to Eris, they'd already traveled much farther in one day than they had in all the weeks past.

Inside the cave, a mound of furry pelts sat near the wall. Eris sorted them into two piles and Jordan quickly realized they weren't just flat furs. Some were stitched into the form of heavy cloaks and coverings for their legs.

"You've been here before," he said, stating the obvious.

"Another of my homes." She flicked her fingers and flames burst from the stone floor. She handed Jordan a cloak and leg coverings. "It gets very cold here, especially at night."

~ 66 ~

Although the air itself seemed to freeze after the sun set and Jordan had never felt so cold in all his years and all his travels, Eris still kept him at a distance. They lay on opposite sides of the fire under the heavy furs and she continued her on-going explanation about the creatures that made up the Daemoni. Besides vampyres and mages, the Ancients had created shifters or, as Eris sometimes called them, Weres. A number of Ancients had taken the bodies of every kind of predatory animal that lived on Earth and, using their unearthly powers, created beasts that could transform into human shape and back again.

"You have encountered one," she said. "A werewolf. Your sister's friend almost killed him."

"That was a werewolf?" Jordan asked. *I was right! It wasn't a normal wolf.*

"The Daemoni have been living among humans since nearly the beginning of time. People who disappear, seemingly lost in the woods or wilderness...they become food. Or sometimes one of us. A vampyre or shapeshifter, that is. No human can *become* a mage. We are born."

"Vampyres and shifters are not?"

"Weres can be born, but they can also be created through infection of a human. Vampyres can only reproduce by draining a human's blood and then replacing it with some of their own. The human nearly dies and nearly comes back to life. But not all the way."

"Like those soldiers Cassandra saw," Jordan muttered, recalling his sister's story.

"Hmph. Another problem with vampyres. The Ancients want them to keep creating more and battlefields provide perfect opportunities, but they are usually sloppy at it. They shouldn't let their children rise all alone like that. It's too dangerous."

"Are you saying you care about the humans they'll attack?"

"Of course not. I care for our secrecy. Abandoned newborns can ruin us."

The following day, Eris led him again on flashes through the mountains until they appeared on a snow-covered expanse of land bordering a lake so large, Jordan couldn't see the other side. Perhaps it was a sea. He found the whites and blues of the landscape beautiful in a completely opposite way of how he thought of home as beautiful, but he saw no indication of any kind of life—not human or animal or inhuman. At least, not until Eris waved her hands and an entire village suddenly appeared around them.

The village was small, made of several tents encircling an open area where people dressed in furs gathered around a large fire pit in the center.

"Shaman," Eris said, nodding at them. "That's what they call themselves, though they are essentially witches and wizards. Follow me."

She led him into one of the tents made of animal skins stretched over long logs. The tent was barren inside, showing no signs of being used. Jordan wondered if this was another of Eris's homes, but before he could ask, she waved her hands over the center of the floor and a hole opened up before them. Crude stairs carved into the earth descended into darkness. She led him downward.

The stairs became a tunnel that continued down, far below the Earth's surface. Just when Jordan began to tire of this unending descent, the tunnel flattened and opened wider, into a network of caves. The deeper they went, the more Jordan realized it was like an underground city, lit by fires in sconces on the walls and in pits dotting the caverns. People who weren't really human—he could feel the magick crackling in the air— milled about, conversing in languages unfamiliar to him.

In one cave they passed, a pale-skinned vampyre bent over a naked human, his mouth at her throat and his hand between her legs. She didn't struggle, even seemed to be enjoying it, as the vampyre drained her blood. In another cavern, three men sat around a wooden table and gnawed on bones, their teeth scraping and pulling off the raw meat, reminding Jordan of wild dogs consuming their kill. Yet, in others, men and women traded furs and pelts, jewels and other goods, just as they did in the agora back home.

Eris tugged at his hand. He'd slowed, distracted by all the activity, but she told him they still had a ways to go. They left what must have been the city's center, passing more caves, these dark and cold. Moaning, growls and even cries of pain filled the air. Finally, they came to the end of the passage. A heavy wooden door with two beastly men blocked their way. Eris murmured something to them in a language Jordan didn't know and tossed her head toward him. They nodded and one stepped back while the other opened the door.

They passed into a large, circular room with hearths carved into the walls every ten or so strides, fires burning within them. Jordan had never seen flames with such vivid colors of green, purple, pink and blue. In a semi-circle of chairs that looked like king's thrones sat figures covered in black cloaks, hiding their forms and faces. Naked women fed them grapes, wine and even their own blood, holding their wrists to where the figures' mouths were hidden in shadows. The evil power thrummed in the room, almost tangible, giving Jordan a thrill.

"Welcome, Jordan," one of them said, rising from his chair and dismissing the attractive blond who'd been sitting on his lap. "We have been waiting for you."

Eris dipped into a sort of curtsey. "Father."

"Thank you, Eris." The figure removed his hood, revealing a young-looking face with Eris's dark eyes and the white hair of someone very elderly. He eyed Jordan and smiled. A proud smile. "Do you know where you are, Jordan?"

"Hell?"

Someone laughed—one of the cloaked figures standing by a fire. He turned toward Jordan, but kept his hood in place, showing nothing of his face. "Very close, indeed. As close as you can get on this side of the veil between here and the Otherworld. How does that make you feel?"

Jordan lifted his chest, bowing up. "At home, to be honest."

He felt more at home here than he'd ever had with his family. They feared their darkness, tried to hide it, pretended they were something they were not. Made him feel like an outcast of his own kin because he let that darkness show, sometimes even embraced it. Here, he could be himself. Here, he belonged, like he had nowhere before. He felt it in his bones.

"Very good, then. That's what we hoped to hear. But still . . . you must prove yourself worthy."

"Worthy of what?" Jordan asked.

"Worthy of joining us," another figure answered. "This is not a place for weak humans."

"I am not weak and prefer not to be compared to the humans."

"We shall see," Eris's father said. "Do you believe in God? The one God?"

The way he said "one God" sounded as though he mocked the idea.

Jordan cocked his head. "I did before. Then I wasn't sure, until my father shared his truth with me. Proved to me that angels and demons exist, so God and Satan must exist, too. With all I have seen in the world, however, I find it difficult to believe that God truly cares for us."

"Because he doesn't," said someone sitting in one of the thrones. "God only cares for himself. He wants all the glory. He wants all the control. He wants everyone to submit to His will. Bah!"

Noises of disgust and anger filled the room, then quieted when Eris's father, the sorcerer, stepped forward.

"*Our* Lord, however, would be a much better god," he said. "He doesn't want all the glory. He wants his followers to keep it for themselves, to feel pride in their accomplishments and who they are. He doesn't want control, but promises everyone would be allowed to do whatever they want. He will not ask you to submit to his will." The sorcerer continued sauntering toward Jordan as he spoke, his voice slightly rising as his excitement grew. "When God demands everyone to care for others, Our Lord says, 'Why? You need only to care for yourself.' God wants humans to be more like Him, but Our Lord points out the truth—that it's unnatural. Humans *aren't* gods. They should be allowed to be human." He stood right in front of Jordan now and leaned even closer. He dropped his voice to nearly a whisper. "And the inhuman should be allowed to be their natural selves, too."

Jordan's eyes lit up. "I think I like this lord of yours. He is . . . ?"

"Satan, yes," the sorcerer said. "The truly better god. Do you agree?"

Jordan didn't have to think about it for long. The choice was simple. "How can I not agree? He offers so much more."

The figure by the fire moved between two thrones, into the center of the room. He didn't so much as walk as he did glide. More figures rose from the thrones and gathered in the center, too, encroaching on Jordan and Eris.

"He offers *everything*," one said. "Money, land, women . . . *power*. Especially to you, Jordan."

"To me?"

"He's been waiting for you. He was concerned with the prophecy about your mother at first, even sent us after her to prevent her from bearing children, but when he learned she would give birth to you, he realized he'd misunderstood. Your sister means nothing to him. He's no longer worried about her, when we have you."

Jordan's chest rose with pride once again.

"But first you must prove yourself worthy," Eris's father said. "Prove you can be one of us. Have you taken my daughter yet?"

Jordan looked at Eris and back at her father, surprised at

the turn in conversation. "No, sir."

"Why not?"

"She told me she is not that kind of woman and I respected her wishes."

Eris's father laughed. So did several others. Jordan looked at Eris again, expecting her to be blushing. She wasn't. Her eyes glowed with a knowing look. She licked her lips, her tongue running slowly over the full, pink skin.

"How very *human* of you," her father said. He turned toward the others. "I told you he was too weak."

Jordan bowed up again. "I am not *weak!*"

"Then prove it," one of the cloaked figures commanded. "Take her."

"Certainly," Jordan agreed.

"Now. Here," another said.

"Here?" Jordan asked. *In front of them? In front of her own* father?

"Can you take orders or not?" someone demanded.

Jordan looked at Eris again. She stood completely still, her body rigid and her face devoid of any emotion.

"Take her whether she wants it or not!"

"Prove yourself, Jordan, or we have no need for you."

"He's not worthy," Eris's father said dismissively. "Get him out of here. Give him to the wolves."

Fear of being exiled from where he belonged—rejected by his own kind—jolted through his body. *What do I care about Eris?* If forcing his way with her would prove he was worthy and satisfy them, then that's what he would do. He clamped his hand around her wrist and jerked her into his arms. Everyone fell silent. He braced the back of her head, preventing her from turning away from him, and crushed his mouth onto hers.

To his surprise, her lips yielded to his, parted, allowed his tongue into her mouth. He'd been yearning for this moment since he first laid eyes on her, wanting to feel her softness under his fingers, under himself. He grew hard against her belly and she pressed herself against him, making him shudder. She moved her mouth over his cheek and to his ear.

"You have to do this," she whispered, her teeth scraping his earlobe. "Right here. Show them who you are. What you can be."

"How?" he asked, his hand rubbing and squeezing her soft but firm backside as she ground against him.

"Show them the demon within you. Take me. Take me hard."

She stepped back, as if to move away, but her eyes glinted, encouraging him. He grabbed the shoulders of her peplos and jerked outward, tearing it apart and revealing those beautiful breasts that had been teasing him for weeks. He let the fabric drop to the floor and he took in the full gloriousness of her body. The rest of the room disappeared. He forgot about everyone else, her beauty completely consuming him. He tore off his own clothing and her eyes devoured him. Her lips curled just slightly, enough for him—but no one else—to see the invitation.

And he took her hard, just as she said. He took her every way possible, making her beg and moan and scream his name, until both of them collapsed in a pile of panting satisfaction.

"You did it," she whispered against his ear.

"Very good!" her father said from some distance, clapping his hands. Reality filtered its way back into Jordan's world, reminding him they were not alone. "I've never seen anyone make Eris reach such heights. Very impressive."

Jordan's pride swelled. He had an urge to rise to his feet and strut around the room, displaying his manliness to the women and the men . . . to the *demons*.

"You've passed this test," said one of the others. "But this is only the beginning."

Chapter 7

Cassandra's mind wandered just as much as her feet did as she walked up the rough terrain of the hill, thinking how vast the world was, how she could travel for days or longer without crossing paths with another person. In the last several months, since leaving behind the hut—and the frightening creatures in those woods—the only human contact she'd had was when she stumbled upon battlefields. She treated the injured, as always, then moved along before anyone could capture her.

Just as she avoided forests, especially at night, she also avoided every village, giving them wide berths as Father had done when they moved, but with a clearer understanding of why. Niko—who had slipped away while she slept the night she'd rejected him—had implanted in her a fear of the marketplace that neither Jordan nor Father had been able to do. She'd never felt so alone.

Well, except for Fig, whose rope she gave a tug.

"Come on, Fig, we're almost over the top and we can see what's on the other side. Then I promise we can eat."

The black goat tore another clump of grass and looked up at her, blades disappearing into her mouth as she chewed. Cassandra found her months ago, tangled in a dead fig tree and the weeds growing around it. She'd been bleeding from many gashes, her front leg broken and her eyes already glassy. Anyone else would have put her out of her misery, but Cassandra saw injuries she could heal, the promise of milk and cheese and, even better, companionship for the first time since Niko left. So she freed the nanny, hauled her to the cave she'd stayed in for most of the winter and nursed her back to health.

"*You* can eat, anyway," Cassandra corrected herself as she tugged again on the rope. "I'm all out of food and don't share the same taste for grass and weeds as you."

She'd made it through winter, barely, surviving off the occasional small animal she'd been able to hunt and Fig's milk and cheese. The earth was just now beginning to green again, but her edibles were not yet ripe for picking, except for a few early berries she'd found. And already eaten. What she ached with longing for was bread—for the feeling of mixing the grain and oil between her fingers, for the savory smell as it cooked, for the warmth and satisfaction only bread could provide to the mouth and belly. She hadn't had a bite of bread since the night she'd crushed a beautiful man's heart.

While her body craved bread, her soul yearned for Niko. Too often she questioned her decision in sending him away. Her head knew it was best for both of them, but her heart felt differently. It had wanted to chase after him that next morning when she awoke and he was already gone. It wanted to feel his arms around her again and the jolt through her lips when he brushed them with his. She hadn't gone a day without thinking about him and wondered if he ever thought about her.

"There you go again," she admonished herself as she always did when her mind found its way back to him. "He has a life. There's no reason he'd be thinking of you, unless with anger and disgust. He offered everything to you and you turned your back on him."

Fig bleated at her, surely recognizing this same diatribe Cassandra always gave herself, probably seconding her opinion or telling her to quit thinking about him.

"You're right, Fig. There must be something else to think about," she agreed just as they crested the hill. She sucked in a breath. "Oh! Well. Look at that."

A village spread out from the bottom of the hill. Cassandra hadn't noticed the usual indications—nearby fields, flocks of sheep or worn down paths—and hadn't expected to come so close to a town. Her eyes followed the hills in the half-ring around the valley and she blew out the breath with annoyance. The only way to skirt the town at a safe distance was to turn back the way they'd come and follow the base of the hill and the next one, entering the valley on the far side. At least a day's worth of walking and it was already afternoon.

She dropped the goat's lead, shrugged off the bags and pouches that contained her few belongings and plopped onto the ground under a stand of cypress trees. She meant to think about what she would do next, but her mind kept wandering to the village. To the grain and olive oil she could buy to make bread. To the fresh cloth to replace her raggedy peplos. To new sandals she needed before another strap broke on hers and she was forced to go barefoot. To the marketplace she knew she should avoid but wondered how much longer she really could. There were just some things she couldn't find in the wild and without Father or Jordan to bring them to her, she had no other options. If only she had something worth trading . . . and the courage to even go down that side of the hill.

Voices jerked her out of the internal debate and her head snapped in their direction. Two figures had crested the next hill over, heading down toward the town—a young boy and a man. They were too far away to hear words, just sounds floating on the air, but one of the voices almost sounded familiar. Cassandra squinted her eyes, focusing on the man. Her heart stuttered. *It can't be. I don't know anybody, but I know him!*

She knew the way his hair fell into his face, the way he held his broad shoulders, the confident stride of a warrior. *But how could it be?* She'd just been thinking about how wide and far the earth stretched, how she hadn't seen a person in weeks, how she'd avoided village after village. And now, at the first town she even thought about approaching, the first person she saw besides injured soldiers was one of only two people she actually knew on this earth. One of two people she couldn't stop thinking about.

Without a thought, she somehow had her bags loaded on her back and shoulders and Fig's lead in her hand. Her feet moved halfway down the hill before her brain realized what she was doing. She opened her mouth to call out—

"I wouldn't," came a voice from behind, making her jump. *And that's the only other person I know in this world.* "It's a dangerous place down there for a woman."

Cassandra spun around.

"Jordan," she shrieked. Pulling Fig with her, she ran back up and into his open arms. "What are you doing here? How long have you been here and didn't say anything? How did you even find me?"

He chuckled at all her questions, but only answered one. "We are twins. We have a special connection, no?"

She laughed into his shoulder, giving him another squeeze, not thinking about how she hadn't felt a connection to him in years. Nor about the circumstances of the last time they saw each other.

She stepped back and drank him in with her eyes, but as she did, she noticed something different about him. And not just by sight, but by feeling. He seemed . . . darker, somehow. He was still blond and blue-eyed, of course, but he seemed to be shadowed. By what, she didn't know, but she didn't like the feel of it. She forced her next words out, sure she didn't really want to know the answer. "Where have you been?"

Jordan's eyes lit up brightly, like they always did when he told his stories of adventure. "I found others, Cassandra. I found where we truly belong."

"Others? You mean—"

"Yes, like us."

"There are really others like us?"

"Not exactly like us, but similar. You should see what they can do. They have many more abilities than we do."

"Where are they? How did you find them?"

Jordan pressed his lips together, hesitating. "Do you remember the men I told you about? The ones you called demons?"

She gasped. "The *demons?*"

"No, not them. I found others, some like them and some not. But they're not really demons. They have demon blood, just like us, but also different—"

"Of course they're different! Because we *aren't* demons. Do you really still believe that?"

"More than ever. You need to meet them, Cassandra. They're not what you think. Father lied. They're so much better—better than humans, better than angels, better than anything. They have powers and magick . . . what?"

Cassandra's eyebrows shot up. "*What?* I can't believe you're saying this!"

Jordan grinned. "I know. It's much to accept. But I've seen it myself. I'm *living* it. And they're promising everything. I'll become one of their best warriors and when I do, they say they'll give me everything I've ever wanted. And they will for you, too."

Cassandra shook her head and opened her mouth, but Jordan didn't let her speak.

"You're my sister. They'll see greatness in you, too. I'll make sure of it." He took her hands into his. "This is the way it should be. The life we *should* have. We deserve more than living in the wilderness, hiding from the humans. *They* should be hiding from *us.*"

Cassandra jerked her hands from his grip. He'd spit out the word "humans" as if it tasted badly in his mouth. As if he weren't one. She didn't know what the demons had done to her brother, but she didn't like this Jordan at all. She needed to hang onto him, keep him from going back.

"Jordan, you don't really believe that, do you? I mean, you can't really still believe that we're . . ." She had to force herself to say it. ". . . that we're demons?"

"I don't believe. I *know*," he growled. "I've never felt like I belong anywhere more than when I'm with them, fighting with them, part of them. It's who we are, little sister. And they have so much to offer us—wealth, power—it's where we belong. Come with me and see for yourself."

Cassandra lifted her arm up, indicating the wild. "This is where we belong. In this life *I'm* living, just as Father had raised us, just as we've always lived. Why don't you come with me?"

"This is not the life meant for us. Don't you understand? Father lied to us."

"Jordan! How can you *say* that? Father always—"

"Always thought he needed to protect us, but instead he kept us from being who we're meant to be. He lied about almost everything. I've found the truth!"

Scrutinizing her brother's face, she realized he truly believed that. Was there anything she could do to change his beliefs? She didn't know. All she could do was try to keep him with her, away from those others.

"I don't know what you've found, Jordan, but I've missed you so much. Please don't go back. Stay with me."

"Just let me show you," he said. If she didn't know him better, she'd have thought he actually begged her, but Jordan didn't beg for anything.

"I'm not interested," she said. She turned back toward Fig, who'd been busy chewing up the green buds on a bush, and the sight of the village below surprised her again. With her back to it, all her attention on her brother, she'd forgotten it was down there. *Who* was down there. It didn't matter anymore. She had nothing to trade and even if she did, not in this town. As much as she'd wanted to see that other familiar face again, it wasn't the right thing to do. It would only renew the pain in her heart.

"I saw that," Jordan said, his voice accusing as though she'd just committed some crime.

"What?" she asked, turning back toward him.

"That look. I saw you watching him earlier. You would have followed him if I hadn't stopped—" Jordan cut himself off, looked at the village and then back at Cassandra. His eyes narrowed. "So that's the real reason, isn't it? Why you won't come with me? You still *want* him, don't you?"

Cassandra jerked back, as if he'd slapped her, just as she'd done the last time he'd accused her. The words still stung just as painfully.

"How dare you. After all this time!" Her hands itched to punch him again, but she wouldn't let herself. She wouldn't allow herself to live with that guilt again. She picked up her bags and Fig's rope and pulled the goat as she stalked off, in the opposite direction of the village. She wasn't even a quarter of the way down the hill when Jordan called after her.

"I'm sorry," he said and she stopped in her tracks, disbelieving her own ears. *Did Jordan just apologize? The man who never said sorry?* "I truly am. Let me make it up to you."

"How? Offering me money and power I don't want?"

He stepped in front of her, but she stared at the ground. "I know you don't want it. You're right. *This* is your life. At least let me take you into the agora. If you go with me, they won't harass you and you can collect the supplies you need."

She looked up at him and choked back her shock. He looked sincere. He really meant it. She sighed.

"I have nothing to trade."

Jordan glanced at the goat and back at her.

Cassandra gasped. "I'm not trading Fig!"

"Fig?" Jordan rolled his eyes. "You shouldn't have named her. She's valuable."

"She's very valuable to *me*. She's been my only companion since you left." Of course, that wasn't exactly true. Niko had stayed for nearly two months longer, but she didn't have a problem laying the guilt on her brother. It was better than punching him. "Besides, her milk and cheese probably saved me this winter. I need her."

Jordan grunted. "Fine. I have a few things I can trade for you."

Cassandra glanced down at the town and pressed her lips together. "Can we go to another village?"

"The next one with a decent market is three days away. If you want me to go with you, we go to this one. Here." He unwrapped the himation from his shoulders and draped it over her head. "This will disguise you. Just keep your head down."

As they entered the town's gates and passed house after house, Cassandra marveled at the structures. She'd never been this close to a real house, made of large stones and tiled roofs, some of them nearly three times as tall as Jordan. Mother had told her about growing up in a real home, with a kitchen, bedrooms and a courtyard. About how the women stayed to the kitchen or the back rooms, while her father and other men socialized in their front room. When their house burned down, killing everyone but her—only because she'd been allowed to go care for an ailing neighbor—she'd realized even a comfortable, stone home couldn't protect you from everything. She always said love and family were much more important than a house with many rooms. Cassandra now understood. How could you feel love and the bonds of family with everyone so separated?

Realizing she'd fallen far behind Jordan, she hurried along and caught up to him just in time. They'd entered the marketplace and she didn't want to be too far from him. She kept her head down, following him from stall to stall as he looked for the supplies she needed. They finally stopped at a stand of grain and oils and she listened carefully to how Jordan negotiated and handled the trade, just in case she ever had the courage to do this on her own. Her mouth watered the whole time for the bread she couldn't wait to make. He handed her the goods and she stored them in one of her bags.

She looked up to follow him to the next stall, but he was no longer there. He'd already moved on. But about thirty paces away were Niko and the little boy. She couldn't tear her eyes away, watching as he talked to a merchant standing next to a cart piled high with stones—large ones, big enough for two or three people to stand on, like those used to construct the houses. The little boy squatted next to the wheel of the cart, apparently inspecting a pebble or bug. Who was he?

The answer nearly knocked her to her knees. *Niko lied to me. He's already married. Even has a son!* What had he been thinking? Was he one of those men Jordan once spoke of, who took multiple wives? Did he think she would just accept that without being forewarned? Her chest heaved.

She turned, finding Jordan on the other side of the market, talking to a blond merchant—of course he had found the only other woman in the entire agora. The woman glanced at Cassandra and flicked her hand in the air.

Then something moved in the corner of Cassandra's eye—an unnatural movement that caught her attention. Her head jerked to the left. The top stone on the cart teetered, as if being shaken. Then it tottered . . . slid . . . gained downward momentum . . . right toward Niko's little boy.

"*No,*" Cassandra silently screamed.

Jordan was too far away, even as fast as he was. It was up to her. Dropping Fig's rope, she streaked to the cart, catching the stone just inches above the boy's head, letting out an "oomph!" as she did. It rocked her on her feet, but she caught her balance, steadied herself. The boy flew to Niko's side and stared at her with wide eyes. Niko hadn't even turned, hadn't even noticed that everything had almost gone terribly wrong.

She didn't notice that it already had—for her.

"How, in the name of Zeus, did you do that?" a man bellowed from behind her. She turned, still holding the stone, to find a large man covered in dark hair and beard, staring at her. "It takes three men to move one of those and you—" His eyes bugged, as if he'd really just noticed *her*, not what she'd done. "You're a woman!"

Cassandra swallowed hard. Her whole body started shaking. She glanced around for Jordan, but couldn't see him anywhere, nor the blond merchant-woman. She lowered the stone to the ground, ducked her head and turned back toward Fig, who waited patiently, chewing her cud. A strong hand on her shoulder spun her back around.

"Who are you? Where's your master?" the burly man demanded.

"I-I d-do not—" Her throat constricted, making her stammer. "I-I am not a s-slave."

His eyes narrowed. Three more men came over to join him.

"Then what are you doing in the agora?" another asked. "The only women allowed here are slaves."

Cassandra looked around again with desperation. *Where is Jordan?* But still, he was nowhere to be seen.

"I came with my brother," she said.

"Your brother allowed you to come here? Where is he?" The first man looked around, then called out, "The brother of this woman must retrieve her now."

Cassandra's heart pounded in her chest. Her stomach squeezed and bucked and bile jumped into her mouth. *Where is he?* Jordan never came forth.

"You're a liar," one of the men said. "You're a runaway, aren't you? We don't allow that here. We'll keep you until your master comes."

The first man grabbed her upper arm, pulling the himation off her head, and jerked her toward him.

"No! I'm not a slave. I have no master," she cried out, struggling against his grip.

"Then I'll be your master," he growled.

"No, please. My brother—"

The man tightened his grip and yanked her again. "When my slaves lie to me, they receive the hardest punishment."

"I'm not lying. He's here!" And just as she said it, she saw Jordan standing in the shadows between two buildings, the blond woman with him. She locked eyes with him, hers begging him to help her. With a slight shake of his head and a smirk, he turned and sauntered away.

Her heart stopped cold. He was allowing this to happen. Allowing her to be taken as a slave. Was that his solution so he wouldn't have to worry about her anymore? Or his punishment for not going with him?

As the man dragged her along, past Fig, the goat nudged her hand, pushing her fingers into a fist. Could she hit this man? Hard enough to make him release her? It would draw even more attention, but she could easily escape. No one but Jordan could catch her and he had abandoned her. Again. It was her only way to escape. She tightened her fist, pulled back and just as her knuckles crashed into the man's ribs, someone else called out.

"Wait! She's telling the truth. She's not a slave."

The man released her, but not because of Niko's words. Because of the force with which she'd hit him—he flew to the ground, landing hard on his large rump. His face turned purple with rage. Cassandra looked from her near-captor to Niko, her eyes wide with disbelief and terror. She should run, she knew. But she couldn't release herself from Niko's green-eyed gaze.

"How do *you* know?" the man growled from the ground.

Niko swallowed. He tore his eyes from hers and stared down the man. "Because she is my master."

Chapter 8

Jordan didn't go far—just around the building to another shadow, where he could watch as they captured his sister. Inga, the witch who'd made the stone fall, had already disappeared, waiting for him at a nearby creek. But he couldn't leave yet, too delighted with his work, needing to see it to the end.

Except this man was about to ruin everything. Why had he ever bothered saving him from the werewolf?

"You're not a slave, Niko. You're a soldier," said the man who Cassandra had punched as he struggled to rise to his feet. When he did, he lifted his chest, likely trying to make people forget a woman had knocked him down. "You just want to take her from me."

Niko bent over and whispered something to the boy by his side. The boy ran off, then Niko spoke, his voice firm and convincing. "When I was gone all that time, I was with her. She saved my life, nursed me back to health. I am forever indebted to her. But I ran away and she is here to reclaim me."

Jordan could see the surprise all over Cassandra's face. He shook his head. If this all worked as he'd planned, when he rescued her from her enslavement, the first thing he needed to do was teach her to be a better liar. But this was not going as planned. Not at all.

"You indebted yourself and ran away?" the man demanded. "You ought to be stoned."

"Yes," someone called from the crowd that had begun to gather. "You shame your family and your town!"

The corners of Jordan's lips turned up. *Maybe it will work out after all. Perhaps even better than planned.* But Cassandra surprised him.

"No," she said, her voice loud and firm. She'd recovered from being dragged, now standing with her back straight and putting on the façade of someone in a higher class than she was. "He is my slave. I will take care of the punishment."

Protests came from the crowd, but they were quickly quieted. To Jordan's dismay, both Cassandra and Niko were allowed to leave . . . as long as Niko left with her. He watched as Cassandra grabbed the goat and Niko's arm, and pushed her way through the crowd and out of town. Then he followed.

He momentarily wished Eris were there to cloak him. Inga could cloak herself—make herself invisible—but her magick lacked the strength to hide others. Eris had no idea he was here, though, and wouldn't be pleased about it. In fact, she would be beyond angry, especially in her current condition.

So he followed at a distance, keeping to the shadows as the sun fell in the late afternoon sky. Neither Cassandra nor Niko said a word until they crested the same hill where Jordan had found her and were halfway down the other side. Then Cassandra suddenly stopped and turned on Niko.

"How could you do that?" she demanded, her eyes flashing with anger. Jordan watched with anticipation, hoping his sister would do the right thing and rid herself of this useless man.

Niko appeared unfazed. "You saved my life. I just saved yours. Well, at least, I saved you from a life of enslavement."

"You lied to them!"

"I didn't exactly lie. I *am* indebted to you."

She crossed her arms over her chest and stared at the soldier. "Well, your debt is paid. You can go."

"No. I can't."

"Yes, you can. Go." She flipped her hands at him in dismissal. "Go back to your life. To your wife and children."

"I can't go—" Niko stopped. His brows pushed together. "What do you mean, my wife and children?"

Cassandra lifted an eyebrow. "Your son?"

"I have no—you mean that boy? He's my nephew."

Jordan's eyes narrowed as he saw relief overcome his sister's face, exposing her true feelings for Niko. Now he understood why she'd been so eager to avoid the man.

Cassandra quickly recovered. Her face went stony again. "It doesn't matter. You have a mother to take care of. Sisters. Other family. Go back to them, Niko. Go back where you belong."

"Don't you see that I can't?"

"Of course you can. You're not really my slave."

Niko shook his head. "You don't understand. That's not how it's done here. My own neighbors will stone me, possibly to death, if I don't meet my obligations. You are my obligation now. I just made it public. I must go with you."

Cassandra heaved a breath of frustration. Her eyes flashed again, exciting Jordan with their anger. He hoped she would punch the man, just as she'd hit him.

But her head dropped and her next words came out softly.

"How can you even want to be with me? Didn't you see what happened in there?"

Yes! Jordan fought the urge to whoop aloud. His attention had been consumed with the slavery part of his plan, and how wrong it had gone. He had nearly forgotten about the other part—expose his sister as the demon she really was.

Niko chuckled. "Quite impressive. You took down a grown man."

Cassandra's head jerked up. Her eyes hardened. "And caught a falling stone that he said took three men to carry."

"And protected my nephew. Saved his life. I owe you for that now, too."

Cassandra's eyes widened briefly and then narrowed. "And you don't have a problem with that? You don't think I'm . . . I'm a . . ."

"A what?"

She ducked her head. Her voice softened again, to nearly a whisper. "A demon?"

To Jordan's surprise, Niko laughed out loud. "A demon? As in a spirit? You look quite real and human to me."

Jordan cocked his head. How had he not thought of this before? He'd been around the worshippers of the gods and goddesses enough to know their beliefs. To know that demon, to them, only meant spirit, neither good nor evil. Why hadn't he realized this before? Then the answer hit him. Another lie of Father's he'd fallen for. People wouldn't think them demons if they saw his family's unusual abilities, not in the land where they lived. Farther east, where the Jews lived, perhaps, but not here. These people didn't even have a word for what Jordan now knew as the real demons.

Disgusted with himself for his mistake—he needed a better argument to win over his sister—with Cassandra for her stupidity and with the man who had ruined everything, Jordan flashed away, grateful the Ancients had given him the magick to do so.

"Well?" Inga asked when he appeared at the creek where she waited.

The young witch was already in her preferred state of undress, her light hair falling over her shoulders and brushing the tips of her small, pink nipples. She sauntered up to him and stroked her finger across his downturned mouth.

"Didn't go as planned?" she asked.

"Not exactly. I—"

Inga let him say no more. She grabbed the back of his head, pushed herself against him and crushed her mouth to his. He let her kiss away his anger. He needed this, the distraction she offered. His hands slid along the soft contours of her body and down to her thighs. He lifted her up and she pulled his chiton out of the way as she wrapped her legs around his waist. He lost himself inside her, enjoying her succulent body, feeling no guilt.

He and Eris had brought Inga into their home for both of their pleasures. Eris didn't mind his being with Inga as long as she participated, as well. The larger Eris's belly swelled with baby, though, the less Jordan wanted anything to do with her. Sometimes she would watch Jordan and Inga together. Other times she would fly into a jealous rage. He stayed with Eris, though, and not just because of the baby, but because her magick was unusually powerful and he needed her. And he knew she stayed with him for nearly the same reason—because of his own potential for power.

"I need to get back to Eris," Jordan said later as they rinsed off in the stream. "She'll be giving birth any time now."

Inga trailed a finger over his broad chest. "Are you actually worried about her?"

Jordan chuckled. "You know me better than that. And you know her better than that. She can handle childbirth. I just don't want to deal with the wrath of Eris because I wasn't there."

"I guess I can't blame you," Inga said with a reluctant sigh. Then she gave him an understanding smile. "I'll see you soon."

She disappeared with a faint popping sound. Jordan waded out of the water, let himself dry before dressing, then he flashed home.

"You smell like Inga," Eris said as soon as he entered the small home she had brought him to the night they met. She sat on one of the oversized pillows, her disgusting belly resting between her open legs. Her nostrils flared and her eyes narrowed. "And someone else. Another woman. Who have you been with, Jordan?"

He didn't know how to answer her, because he didn't know if she'd be glad that he hadn't actually been with another woman or angry that he'd found his sister. The closer she came to giving birth, the harder and faster her moods swung. He braced himself and told her the truth.

"*Cassandra?*" she spewed, as if the name tasted as bad as her brews. "Why, Jordan? Why would you risk that?"

He stood there, silently growing angry himself. Why should he have to explain himself to her?

"You know the Ancients want nothing to do with her," Eris said, struggling to push herself to her feet. "She's useless to us. You risk everything by exposing yourself to her. And who else did you risk? Inga?"

"Like you care about Inga," Jordan snapped.

"You'll ruin us," she yelled. "We have so much to gain if you just do what the Ancients want. We can have *everything*. But you'll ruin it all because of your asinine sister!"

Jordan's fist balled at his side and he raised it into the air. Eris's eyes hardened, as if daring him. He wanted to hit her to shut her up because he knew she was right. He *had* risked everything. And only because of his inexplicable need to prove himself right to Cassandra. To prove to her that she's not all good and great and *angelic*.

Eris stared at his fist, but before either of them moved, liquid splashed at her feet, surprising them both. More trailed down her leg and he twisted his lip in a disgusted smirk as his fist fell to his side.

"Never thought I'd see the powerful Eris be so overcome by fear," he said and he turned for the door. "Clean yourself up, woman. I'll be back ... later."

"Jordan," she gasped.

Something in her voice felt wrong. It wasn't fear. Nor a plea to stay. It was ... different. He turned back to her and her eyes were wide, her hands at her enlarged belly. She gasped again and doubled-over. Strong, icy Eris was in pain. They both forgot their anger as Jordan helped her lay down and then flashed to retrieve Inga, who'd promised to help bring his child into the world.

Chapter 9

"You don't believe in demons?" Cassandra asked with disbelief . . . and a little hope. She hadn't expected this, although it occurred to her now if Niko didn't believe in angels, he wouldn't believe in their opposites either. His lack of belief would give her time to convince him she wasn't evil, a chance she never thought she'd have once he knew she wasn't who he thought she was. "How do you explain what I did then?"

Niko shrugged. His eyes were alight, never moving away from her, as if he couldn't get enough of the sight of her.

"I'd say you're a descendant of the gods. It's the only way to explain it." He stepped closer to her, right in front of her, sending her heart into a gallop. His voice came out low, silky. "You are beautiful enough to be."

She looked into his eyes and all those feelings she'd been suppressing rushed to the surface. She wanted nothing more than to be in his arms. And he accepted her! Didn't believe her to be a demon! She couldn't have hoped for this. But . . .

She swallowed. "Niko, you need to go home. You have a life here."

"I told you. I don't. My life is with you now. This is what I want. What I've wanted since the day I left you." He reached out with his hand, cupped it to the side of her face, making her skin tingle.

She laughed nervously. "To be my slave?"

He smiled. "If that's what it takes. I haven't stopped thinking about you, Cassandra. Ever since I returned, they've been harassing me to choose a wife. Fathers have their daughters ready and they'll deliver. Young girls, thirteen, fourteen, hardly any older than my nieces. The thought disgusts me. But I never really had a choice. Not since I met you."

"I can't live like your women do. Jordan told me how you hide them. They can't leave their homes or even go outside. You know I can't do that."

"I do know. You're free and strong and . . . just different from any woman I know. And that's what I love about you."

Cassandra blinked.

"Yes. I love you. I want to be in your life, whatever, however it is. I will follow you wherever you go. I will stay with you as long as you will have me. Just, please, don't say no again. Don't tell me you can't. I understand you *are* different, very different. But you don't need to hide. Not from me."

His eyes were pools of warm water, the color of the sea, and she felt herself falling into them. Falling into him. When he leaned over, she didn't back away. When his lips brushed hers, she didn't push him off. When they pressed harder, she kissed him back. She pushed her hands through his dark hair to the back of his neck and pulled herself against him. His strong arms wound around her, holding her tightly, the feeling she'd been yearning for all winter long. Her lips parted, letting him in. She tasted the sweetness of grapes on his tongue and wanted more.

More of him. More of his touch. Warmth spread throughout her body and her lower belly tightened. Her thighs trembled.

She reluctantly pulled away and just stared at his face, the face she loved, until she recovered and could speak again.

"It's getting dark. We should find a place for camp, don't you think?"

His mouth pulled into a wide grin and his eyes glinted. He understood.

With little light left to find anything better, Cassandra led Niko back to the cave she had slept in last night. He collected firewood along the way and built them a fire while she tied Fig to a tree just outside. She didn't get new linen for a peplos or new sandals, but she did get grain and olive oil so she was able to make the bread she'd been craving so much. It was all they had to eat, but she had what she wanted—her body had bread and her soul had Niko.

They lay down on the single fur pelt she had, pressing together so they could both fit, and she realized her body really wanted Niko, too. Her heart pounded against her chest and against his, too, as he pulled her into his arms and kissed her. The passion rose just as quickly as before, perhaps because it had never entirely left. She kissed him back with a fervor she didn't know she had, tasting his lips, his tongue, his skin as their mouths moved over each other's faces.

Her hands slid through his hair as his moved over her back, down her side, along her thigh. He kissed her jaw line, her throat, her collarbone. She gasped as he moved to her breast, kissing her hardened nipple through the peplos. Her body felt hot and shaky. Her breasts felt tight and ached for another touch. As if knowing what she wanted, his hand gently squeezed the fullness, his thumb ran over the nub and then he pinched it, making her moan. In one swift movement, he had her belt undone and her peplos over her head. She quaked as his appreciative gaze slid over her naked body.

His fingers brushed between her breasts, made circles

around her belly, making it quiver. They came back up and cupped her breast as his mouth lowered to it. His tongue flicked her nipple, rolled it around and then his mouth clamped down and it felt as though he sucked a line that came straight from her groin. Another moan escaped her lips.

He moved his mouth to her other breast as his hand glided along her body, stroking heat that spread along her skin. He slid his hand under her, along her backside and thigh, down to her calf. He hitched her leg over his hip and she felt him hard and hot against her. He moaned at the touch. And in another swift motion, his chiton was off and Cassandra drank in the sight of his bare body.

Their mouths moved together, against each other, kissing, licking, sucking. Their hands explored each other's bodies, learning the dips and rises and curves, their breathing becoming ragged. After a moment's hesitation, she took him in her hand and found him rock hard. He throbbed against her as she stroked and Niko moaned.

They played with each other, teasing, testing their boundaries. Cassandra knew nothing about this intimate activity, but she knew he belonged inside her. And she couldn't stop thinking about it. His fingers weren't enough. She wanted *him*. She cried out for him, begged him. She expected it to hurt—he was so big and she was so tiny—and it did. But only for a few moments. Then the promise of what was to come, what he had already brought her to with just his hand and mouth, eliminated the pain.

She rose against him. He shoved farther inside her. He pulled out slightly and pushed in again, even deeper. She fell into the rhythm with him, pushing and pulling, rocking her hips, squeezing around him. He groaned. She moaned. They moved faster and harder. He thrust deep inside her and she begged him to do it again. And he did. Again and again. Her whole body wracked with pleasure. The next time he did it, it knocked the breath out of her. She soared into another place, a place of thorough bliss. Her back arched off the ground. Her toes curled. She screamed. She tightened against him. He made several quick, short thrusts and convulsed inside her with a long groan.

They fell back, panting, their arms wrapped tightly around each other. She shuddered several times and so did he. As soon as he rolled off her, she missed him. She wanted to be pressed against him again. She wanted him to be inside her again. And soon enough, he was.

❦

As she and Niko began their life together, Cassandra had to adjust to having a man with her again, as well as adjust to the fact that he wasn't her father or brother but her lover. He took care of more than her basic needs for survival and companionship. They lived as husband and wife, moving around as she always had, and she imagined this was what it was like for Mother and Father before she and Jordan were born. She better understood now why they looked at each other as they did, why Father had changed when Mother died. She didn't even want to think about when that time would come for her, which would be inevitable—she would outlive Niko. She focused instead on the present, on the love she thought she would never be able to have.

Niko still had days of fatigue, remnants of the wolf attack, though not as often as before. The army had dismissed him, though, not needing a weak soldier. He'd told her how difficult it had been to accept at the time. At least, until she returned to his life and filled the void.

Their hardest struggle at first, however, came with the summer heat. Cassandra had never felt so miserable, didn't remember it bothering her so much. She felt sick and unable to eat much of the time. She'd taught Niko about edible plants and fruits and always double-checked his gatherings, just to be safe. Thinking the animals in that part of the land were contaminated, they moved on. With the end of summer, however, the sickness had passed and they understood. Her belly swelled with baby. Six months later, she gave birth in a cave by the sea.

"You are so pretty, Andronika, just as beautiful as your mother," Niko cooed at the baby, sliding his finger over her cheek. He looked up at Cassandra. "In my old life, they often left baby girls at the doors of rich men to be raised as slaves."

"They didn't want daughters?"

"They can't work like sons can. Many families can't afford to feed them when they would receive nothing in return."

Cassandra frowned. "That's ridiculous. Daughters are just as precious as sons!"

Niko smiled down at Andronika. "Even more precious, right, my angel?"

Cassandra's frown turned into a smile. She'd yet to convince Niko of one God, Satan, angels and demons, but perhaps there was still hope.

She was glad Niko loved their daughter so much because she never did bring him a son. She had been surprised enough to even be able to have Andronika at her age.

Time passed. Andronika grew. Niko began showing signs of age—a few gray hairs, lines around his eyes. Cassandra didn't.

Shortly after Andronika's ninth birthday, they stumbled onto a battlefield, the second one in two days. The fight had been over and all live soldiers already rescued, but the dead had not yet been retrieved. And there were many. The fighting had become more intense, evidenced by the number of fields of bodies they kept coming upon. And also by the quality of the soldiers.

"This one is too young to be out here," Niko said, indicating a boy who couldn't be more than twelve. He pointed to another body. "That one too old. The army's in bad shape. The Romans are decimating us. We need better men."

Cassandra swallowed down the lump in her throat. She understood his meaning. "Niko—"

"They need me, Cassandra. I owe it to our country. To our people."

She inhaled a deep breath. What could she say? *So do we?* Although it was true, it was selfish. He was a warrior. Raised and trained to be a soldier. Even with the occasional fatigue, he was still stronger than these boys and elderly men. Boys whose mothers would never see them again. Men whose last days had been spent in the misery of war. She gave a sharp nod, turned and returned to Andronika.

But when the time came for Niko to leave, she could no longer hold the tears back.

"I'll miss you, too, both of you," Niko said, hugging them both.

"When will you come back, Father?"

"As soon as I can. Not long, my angel."

Cassandra walked with him, out of Andronika's hearing range. "You *must* come back, Niko. I need you. Andronika needs you. You do what you need to do and then come back to us."

He pulled her into his arms. She pressed her tear-streaked face against his chest.

"Of course. Just don't leave until I do, or I'll never find you."

"We'll be right here."

"And I'll be back."

He kissed her, long and heavy, and she soaked in the feeling, remembering it, hoping it wasn't the last time.

Chapter 10

Jordan spent his years proving himself to the Ancients, doing their fighting and bidding. He learned their ways and their purpose: harvesting human souls for Satan. As Jordan gained the Ancients' approval, they rewarded him with more power. But it still wasn't enough. He wanted what all the other Daemoni had—the strength, endurance, speed and ruthlessness of the Weres; the magick of the mages; and, most of all, the invincibility and immortality of the vampyres. Father's blood was not enough. Father had, after all, died. And Jordan did not want to die. He deserved more.

He and Eris began work on a potion to give him all the best qualities of the others. This was why he needed her—only she could provide the level of magick necessary and she believed in their goal. She was nearly as obsessed as he with his rise to the top, believing he'd take her and their son with him. Of course, he would take Deimos, knowing his son had immense potential to follow in his lead. Eris, on the other hand . . . he hadn't yet decided. She'd been quite useful so far, but would she be once they achieved their goal? He wasn't sure he could trust her then.

He had also become less attracted to her as the years passed. The power she put into the potions drained her and her true age began to show. Her body lost its luscious curves, creases lined her face and her once silky, raven hair was streaked with coarse, gray strands. At the same time, her potions appeared to have stopped him from aging at all. His speed increased, his power grew, his senses became nearly equal to those of the vampyre, and his own appeal and the effect he had on women improved even more. Why should he settle for the old witch Eris when he could have anyone?

For now, he still needed her. Although he had gained many of the others' qualities, he still lacked invincibility and immortality. They continuously tested his skin and it still bled under the blade. Unlike the vampyres, whose skin, he'd noticed, was impossible to penetrate.

"Zardok wants to see you," Eris said as soon as he returned home after several weeks at battle.

"Perfect timing," he muttered. All he wanted to do was clean himself and sleep, but not even he could ignore the summon of Zardok, an Ancient. The magickal pull was very real and physical, like a hook in his gut, reeling him to the Ancients. The longer he waited, the stronger and more painful the pull.

"It is, actually," Eris said, bringing him a bowl of stew. "I believe I've figured out the potion and we just need one more ingredient. Just one and you will have immortality."

"And then you can take over the Daemoni army," Deimos said, appearing in the doorway with a satchel overflowing with herbs. "Just what you've always wanted."

Jordan eyed his son, surprised that he seemed to have grown again just in the short time he'd been gone. Only a few more years and a few more inches and Deimos would be a man. His son sat on the floor next to him and Eris handed him a bowl.

"So what is this one ingredient and what does Zardok have to do with it?" Jordan asked before taking a bite.

"We need his blood," Eris said matter-of-factly.

Jordan spewed stew out of his mouth. Deimos laughed. Jordan ignored him.

"Are you crazy, woman?" he demanded. "He's an Ancient. The most powerful vampyre."

"The *original* vampyre," Eris added. "That's why we need it. We can finish the potion and then you'll be nearly as powerful as the Ancients."

Jordan stared at her for several long moments, not knowing whether to shake some sense into her or admire her for such tenacity. He finally just shook his head.

"How do you expect me to get blood from Zardok? I doubt he'll just give it to me."

"Of course not. But you're clever, Jordan. You'll figure it out, if you want this badly enough."

He growled. She already knew just how badly he wanted it. He would have to find a way.

છ

Zardok scared Jordan, not an easy thing to do. Jordan towered over the vampyre's ancient body, so it wasn't his size, or the stark contrast of his dark hair against his pale, nearly transparent skin or even his red eyes. Just as some people exuded love or anxiety or hostility, Zardok exuded overwhelming terror. With time and his own power, Jordan had learned to block vampyres' powers, so he no longer felt fear when he was around them. Except for Zardok. The vampyre was too old and too powerful—a demon in human form.

Eris had once explained that a true demon offered Zardok,

~ 102 ~

the human, eternal life in exchange for his soul. Zardok had been the leader of his clan and ruled them with cruelty and fear while leading them to attack and destroy other clans. He wanted power over everyone and the demon's offer was one he couldn't reject. He'd be superior to all the others. No one could kill him. He'd rule all the lands. So he surrendered his soul, accepted the evil spirit into his body and transformed. Now, rather than a kingdom of humans, he fathered a family of the fiercest and most dangerous predators on Earth. But they had their problems.

"We need to build our army, Jordan," Zardok said from his throne in the circular room far underneath the Earth's surface. The other thrones sat empty, most of the Ancients absent, except for a few who stood in shadows near the fires. "There is a prophecy that God himself will be coming to Earth in human form. He will be called God's son, if the prophecy is true."

Not all prophecies were, but apparently this one had the Ancients worried.

"So you would like an army who can kill him, defeat God, so Our Lord may reign?" Jordan asked.

Zardok laughed. "We wish it were so simple. Our Lord will use his spirits to try to tempt the son, but we would still not defeat God so easily. Our worry is in the rest of the prophecy—that the son's death will allow humans to give their souls to God by a simple decision. Good deeds, which are so easily thwarted by us now, will no longer be necessary to join God in Heaven. They will simply have to choose to believe in him, accept the son's sacrifice and repent for their so-called sins for Our Lord to lose their souls forever."

"We must keep them from believing then," Jordan said.

"Yes. In case this prophecy comes true. We can kill them before they believe and Our Lord will have their souls. Or we can make them one of us and they can see that Our Lord is the better god."

"You want to convert more humans into Daemoni?"

"Perfect, isn't it? We win their souls and grow our army at the same time and eventually, we rule all humans. They will bow to only us, forgetting their God." Zardok stood and paced, his excitement growing. "Vampyres will create more vampyres. Weres will create more of their own by infecting humans. We will release the bind on mages that prohibit them from mating with humans and allow them to spread their magick. Our numbers will grow until we outnumber humans and those that remain will be our slaves. We will have conquered Earth and God will have no choice but to relinquish his power. Our Lord will win!"

"What about the other gods—Zeus and the others? We will need to defeat them first."

Zardok stopped his pacing and laughed. "There are no other gods. Our Lord sent faeries into this realm to pose as gods and goddesses, distracting the humans and making them unbelievers in the truth. The faeries do it for the attention and adoration."

Jordan pondered this for a moment—first, that faeries existed, which he had not known, and second, the distraction they'd been providing to the very people he had lived among.

"Since they are unbelievers, we should target them first," he said. "I know firsthand they have very strong warriors and they're always fighting each other for power over the land I come from. We should take those soldiers, make them us."

"Excellent idea!" Zardok said, rubbing his long, bony hands together. "Do not forget, however, the strongest of the believers. Turning them from God to us is a dual win."

Jordan bowed his head in agreement. "But what do you want of me?"

Zardok put his hands on Jordan's shoulders and although he'd just been rubbing them together—an action that should have warmed them—their iciness crept right down into Jordan's bones. He fought the urge to shiver. Zardok's red eyes pierced into Jordan's.

"I need you to lead this army."

Jordan's heart leapt but his brow furrowed. This was what he'd always wanted. What he had been working so hard for. But it didn't make sense.

"I thought you would want one of your own to lead."

Zardok let out a frozen sigh against Jordan's face. "My children are the greatest predators. They can be strong leaders, too, but only of themselves. The others will not respect their leadership enough for something so important. We need someone who is not any of them, yet is all of them. We know of your and Eris's potions. We see you taking on qualities of all of us."

Jordan broke the hold of Zardok's gaze, looking past him into a purple-flamed fire. He and Eris had tried to keep their work covert, not knowing what the Ancients' reaction would be. They wanted to wait to show them the results until it was too late for the Ancients to order them to stop.

"We approve of it, Jordan!" Zardok said, shaking him. "We are anxious to see the final outcome. The prophecy said you would lead our army, but we didn't see how, as weak as you were. But look at you now! You and your descendants will be the best of all of us. You are our future."

Jordan held his stony face, even while his heart raced with excitement and even knowing Zardok could not only hear his heart rate but also sense his emotions. He tried to control the urge to celebrate because there was still one missing piece. He inhaled deeply, trying not to gag on the mix of odors in the cavern that left a nasty taste in the back of his throat, and exhaled slowly, gathering his courage.

"We're not quite there, though," he finally said. "And without this last ingredient, I do not believe your army will respect me. They will see me as too weak to be their leader. Especially your children."

Zardok's back straightened and he lifted an eyebrow. "What ingredient would that be? Surely Eris can get her hands on just about anything."

Jordan crossed his arms over his chest and braced himself, putting forth as much power as he could against this Ancient. "Your blood."

Zardok's eyes widened and glowed a brighter red. Then they narrowed and he rubbed his chin as he seemed to truly consider this.

"What will my blood do for you?" he asked thoughtfully.

"Eris says it will give the final touch to invincibility and immortality. If I can't be killed and I have all the traits of the other creatures, they will *have* to respect and obey me."

Zardok paced again, but this time silently. Jordan stood his ground and waited, watching the vampyre's shadows shift on the wall in the flicker of the various fires. Zardok finally stopped right in front of Jordan.

"I will do it," he said, but Jordan didn't respond, sensing the ultimatum. "But first, you will bring me someone you once cared deeply about. Prove to me one more time that you are worthy."

Jordan's brows pushed together again. "I care about no one. Unless you want my son?"

"No. There is too much potential for your son."

"Eris?"

Zardok rolled his eyes in a very human way. "Her father would never allow it. But I don't want her either. Even if you actually cared for her. I want a human. Someone I can turn."

"I know no humans. The only other would be my sister and I would be happy to bring her to you."

"I don't want you to be *happy* about it," he growled. "That's part of the point. But I don't want your sister, either. Again, she's not human. Not fully. And she's too weak and pathetic. *Human*, Jordan. Bring me a human you and yours have loved . . . and one that would make a great vampyre, possibly as great as me."

"But—"

"If you want my blood, that is my order." Zardok waved his hand, clearly dismissing him. "In the meantime, begin building our army."

☙

Jordan had no idea how to fulfill Zardok's wish. Eris said she could try to create a love potion for him to fall in love with a human, which she only offered because she knew he would have to sacrifice that woman in the end, but she also said love potions never worked. Not truly. And he didn't have time to play such games. He had an army to grow and lead.

Given small numbers of troops at a time—they couldn't turn too many people at once without creating alarm that would sabotage their efforts—Jordan took them to the battlefields, joining in the fights until the last soldier fell and he and his men could pick through those who barely lived. He hand-selected the soldiers he wanted turned and his troops did the biting, the bleeding and the changing. But then he lost them while they took their new children back to teach them their ways and Jordan would have to wait for the next troops to arrive.

He stepped through the sea of bodies after one such battle, wanting to get this over with. He was distracted by the thought of seeing his sister, a thought he hadn't had in years. He'd squelched his need to prove her wrong, nearly forgetting her completely. The Ancients said they had no use for her—too weak to do them any good and Jordan had almost come to believe it. But his conversation with Zardok had sparked an idea. It was time to pay her a visit, let her see what he'd become and finally convince her of the truth. Perhaps after this round left with their newborns, he could find her.

He bent down to a soldier whose chest barely rose and fell and felt for a heartbeat. He was still alive enough to be turned, but as Jordan examined his body, his nose wrinkled. Not a good specimen. Too old and weak. He stood and cast his eyes around, looking for any other signs of life, but there seemed to be none. Until he heard someone choking.

Jordan rushed over to the fallen warrior. His body looked strong and powerful, and, although shallow wrinkles spread from the corners of his closed eyes, the face was not too old for his use. But it was familiar. Jordan knelt down and the man grabbed for his hand, scrunching his eyes shut tighter and pursing his lips against a wave of pain.

"Do you believe in God?" Jordan asked him.

"Zeus," the man gasped, blood bubbling out of his mouth and down his chin. "Unless . . . you can . . . convince me now . . . . My wife . . ."

Jordan was sure he knew his wife. As he studied the man's face, he became more certain of the recognition and an idea occurred to him. This man was a prime candidate for the Daemoni and his soul perfect for their lord. But he could also serve a purpose for Jordan. He cared nothing for this man, but Zardok didn't need to know this. And hurting this man's wife . . . it would be the ultimate revenge and perhaps enough of a sacrifice for Zardok.

"This one," Jordan called out to one of the vampyres. "But not you. Take him to Zardok. Tell him he's from me, what he asked for."

The vampyre lifted the soldier whose eyes popped wide open with terror. And Jordan knew without a doubt this was the man he thought. He knew those eyes and for just a moment, they shared a vision of the woman they both loved. Well, Jordan once loved. A long time ago. He clapped his hand on the man's forehead and slid the lids down, covering those haunting green eyes.

Chapter 11

Cassandra sat on a flat boulder near the edge of a cliff and gazed out at the sea, while her daughter stood behind her, braiding her hair. She stared at an island far off in the distance, near the horizon.

"I think I'd like to live out there," she said, pointing at it. "Away from all the wars and people and on an island all our own. What do you think, Andronika?"

"Are there boys on the island?" her daughter asked.

Cassandra chuckled. *How has she become so interested in boys?*

"No, which is another advantage of living out there," Cassandra said.

"Mother. How am I supposed to meet a husband if we live on an island by ourselves?"

"You have several years before you should even be looking for a husband." Cassandra sighed. "I'm just ready for some peace. The battles have been carrying on my entire life. I see all the soldiers we can't help . . ."

Andronika wrapped her arms around her mother's shoulders. "We've come as far east as we can to get away from them. Unless you want to build a boat? I guess I would go to the island with you, at least until I become a woman. But we have to wait for Father."

Cassandra blinked back the sting in her eyes. They hadn't seen Niko for over a month. He usually returned every few weeks, helping them move and re-settle when necessary, before leaving again for war. Once or twice over the past few years, he'd been away this long, but she'd failed to convince herself he would come back this time, too. Something felt different. But the pain of thinking she'd never see him again would seize her entire body—she felt it threatening to envelop her now and she inhaled deeply, pushing it down.

"Of course we'll wait for your father," she said, standing up. "Come. We must gather some herbs before nightfall."

"You're going to the battlefield, aren't you?"

"From the sounds of it, I don't think the fight will last until morning."

When Niko first left them here, they had been a safe distance away, but the war had moved closer. Cassandra had been hearing the signs of its approach as she explored the area and hunted for supplies. Today's battle was only a short run away. Although her heart ached for peace, she knew her place—healing the wounded.

"Will you take me this time? I can help. You know I can."

Cassandra frowned as she pulled her daughter into her arms. She'd been teaching her everything she knew about healing and Andronika was right—she could help. But Cassandra couldn't stand the thought of the girl seeing so many mutilated bodies, hearing the moans of the dying, feeling the squish of blood-saturated grass under her feet. She was still too young and innocent.

"I know you think you're close to becoming a woman, but you're still a child, and a battlefield is no sight for a child's eyes."

"You're just afraid you'll find Father's body and you don't want me to see that."

Cassandra inhaled deeply, the salty air stinging her nose and coating the back of her throat. "You're right. I don't want you to see that."

Andronika stared at her mother with the same dark eyes they shared and tears pooled then spilled over her cheeks. She buried her face against Cassandra's shoulder. "I don't want to see that either, Mother. He has to come back. He *will* come back to us."

Cassandra only responded by squeezing her daughter more tightly. She wished she could confirm Andronika's plea, but she couldn't. Something was wrong this time. The feeling had intensified over the last few days and she now felt it in her bones. Something was wrong with Niko, but she didn't know how to find him or how to save him.

❦

Mist hung around the trees and hovered over the grass in the pre-dawn light, turning the entire world an eerie gray as Cassandra ran for the battlefield. She headed in the direction where the sounds of yesterday's fighting had come from, but now it was dead silent and she had to hunt for the site. The sun had risen high in the sky when she finally found it.

Her heart sank. Not a single body stirred.

No one screamed or moaned or gasped in pain. No chests rose and fell with even the slightest of breath. She hadn't been able to sleep, worrying about waiting until morning, but she couldn't leave Andronika alone all night long. Now she was too late to be of any use.

Tears streamed down her cheeks as she walked through the

field, checking every single body, just in case she was wrong. Without realizing it at first, she even checked those who were obviously dead, rolling them over if their faces were planted in the ground. Wiping mud away to get a good look at their features. Making sure none of them were Niko. Even with all the death surrounding her, she couldn't help breathing a sigh of relief when she didn't find him after checking every corpse. She didn't know what she would have done if she had. The guilt of not coming earlier, in time to save him, might have killed her.

With slumped shoulders and a slow stride, she began making her way back to the sea and to her daughter. She prayed no one had suffered through the night because she hadn't come sooner. She prayed she'd never have to see another battlefield . . . so much blood . . . so much death ever again.

Cassandra felt the evil presence before she heard the snap of a breaking branch. Her heart jumped. She froze and held her breath to listen. Silence. Except for the racing pulse in her ears. And again she felt . . . evil. Pure evil sliding across her skin like this morning's mist. Without waiting to know what it was, she broke into a sprint.

"Wait! Cassandra, wait," bellowed a man's voice.

Someone grabbed her from behind and she screamed and kicked. A hand clamped over her mouth.

"Little sister, it's just me."

Cassandra's eyes widened. Her heart stopped. She fell still.

Then she blinked, her heart pounded again and she panted against her brother's hand. She squirmed in his arms.

"No more screaming?" he asked. She shook her head and he let her go.

She dropped to her feet and spun on him. Her jaw dropped. *"Jordan?"*

He looked nearly the same as the last time she'd seen him—he hadn't aged a single day—but something in his blue eyes looked different, making them hard and icy. Although no lines creased his skin, his hair had lightened so much, it looked almost white. And there was something different about his face, a new sharpness to his features that made him even more attractive yet . . . frightening. *He was the evil I just felt.* She sucked in a breath at the realization.

"What have you done to yourself?" she asked.

He grinned and it was both familiar and terrifying. "I'm improved. Even better than I was."

"Better?" Cassandra echoed.

"Nearly perfect! I brought you something." He held out his hand, palm up, to reveal two beautiful, gold brooches decorated with blue stones. Jewelry only the wealthiest women would wear.

"How . . . ?"

"Money is nothing to me. I have all the riches I want. All the *power* I want. And you can, too, little sister." He pushed his hand toward her.

She lifted her brows, ignoring the gifts. "Is this what you came for? Have you been hunting me down, just to give me gifts I don't need and to tell me how great you are?"

"Every woman needs brooches for her peplos. And to tell you how great you can be, too."

Cassandra blew out a breath of frustration. "Why can't you ever come see me just to see me, Jordan? It's been . . . I don't know . . . before my daughter was born so thirteen *years*? You left me to become someone's slave, after promising to protect me. And here you are, still saying the same thing you said way back then. You're still stuck on that stupid argument that you won't win because I want nothing to do with you and your friends. I don't care how great you are, I *don't* want to be like you! Why can't you just come and have a normal conversation between a brother and his sister?"

Jordan blinked at her and then his face fell and his shoulders sagged. With a forlorn look, he tucked the jewels into the pouch at his hip. She'd gone too far with him once again. What was it about Jordan that made her snap every time she saw him? She opened her mouth to apologize, but he spoke first.

"Because we're not a normal brother and sister," he said.

Cassandra groaned.

"*I* am normal," she said. "As normal as I can possibly be and that's how I like it, so leave me alone if that's all you're here to harass me about."

She spun on her heel and began running toward home. Jordan suddenly appeared in front of her, just far enough away that she could stop before colliding into him.

"I'm sorry, Cassandra. You're right."

She momentarily forgot what he should be apologizing for, overcome with surprise. "How . . . ? How did you do that?"

His mouth turned up in a slight grin. "It's one of those things I wanted to show you. But not now. You're right. Let's talk."

She crossed her arms over her chest. "About what?"

He shrugged. "About life. How has yours been? It's been a long time since we last saw each other."

She stared at him for a long moment, again in shock. Was he really asking about her? Did he really care? She knew she shouldn't trust him, not after what he did to her last time, but unlike him, she couldn't turn her back on family. She began again for home, but this time walking slowly, Jordan by her side. She told him all about her life and about Andronika, her chest filling with pride for her daughter.

"What about you?" she asked when she finally finished, but then she felt the need to clarify. She didn't want to hear anything about demons. "I mean, do you have a wife? Any children?"

"I have a son, not too much older than your Andronika. He was born the day I last saw you, actually." Jordan told her about his life, including the demons and the Ancients and despite herself, she couldn't help but listen with curiosity. Interest in his life, though, not about them specifically and certainly not about joining them. But when he did start talking about them, she still couldn't bring herself to stop him. *Vampyres? Were-animals? Mages?*

"I've been gaining some of their powers," Jordan said, startling her once again.

"What do you mean?"

"Like what I did earlier, when I appeared in front of you. We call it flashing. Other things . . . magickal things."

"Oh, Jordan, why are you doing this?" she demanded, grabbing his wrist. Ice-cold pain shot into her hand, forcing her to let go. "You'll lose yourself to them. You'll lose your soul!"

He shook his hand, as if her touch had hurt him, too. "My soul is already theirs. And I'm doing it because I believe in them. I believe in Our Lord. He is a better god than your God."

Cassandra gasped. "You mean . . . Satan?"

"Yes. He would—"

"How can you even say that? What are you thinking, Jordan? You need to get out now. I can help—"

"I don't want to get out. It's where I belong. I'm leading them all now, all but the Ancients. And you can't do anything. It's too late. It was too late the day we were born. We *are* demons."

Cassandra shook her head. "Even if you believe you have bad blood, you could choose, Jordan. You could choose to live the rest of your life righteously. God would still forgive you."

Jordan laughed. "Why would I do that? Look at all that I can do!"

He flicked his hand and fire exploded out of it, hitting a nearby log. Then he lifted his finger and the log rose into the air. He made it spin and then sent it flying into a large rock, where it smashed into splinters. He flicked his other hand and doused the fire with a stream of water that flowed from his palm.

"And there's more, so much more. And you can have all this power, too, little sister."

Cassandra stared at him wide-eyed, her heart pounding. Evil waves pulsed off of Jordan's body and when he turned toward her, his eyes were red instead of their normal blue. Her breath caught. She shook her head.

"No," she whispered. "Never. You've gone too far, Jordan."

She broke into a run. Jordan appeared in front of her. She darted to the right. There he was again. She switched to the left but she couldn't get away from him. He just laughed, a maniacal sound she'd never heard from him before. A frightening sound she didn't ever want to hear again.

"Just leave me alone," she yelled.

"Come with me, little sister. Join us and live the life you're *supposed* to."

"You're mad. You are evil, but not because of Father. Because of your own doing!"

He took a step toward her, his eyes filled with malice. Her heart hammered painfully against her ribs. She'd never felt so scared of him before. But this wasn't her brother. Not the Jordan she grew up with.

She lifted a large stone over her head and threw it toward him, not to hurt him but to distract him. He stopped it in mid-air. Not waiting to see if he threw it back at her, she ran again.

The shelter by the cliff came into view and she realized she couldn't bring Jordan to her daughter. He couldn't know where they stayed. So she veered right, ran another two-hundred paces and then stopped dead in her tracks. Jordan appeared right in front of her. They stood in a stand-off, but he didn't move to hurt her.

"Please, Jordan," she begged. "Please just leave me alone. You've done this to yourself, but don't do it to me. Please."

"But *why*? I don't understand you. Why wouldn't you want all this?" He sounded genuinely perplexed, as if the idea of rejecting all he had was absurd. But Cassandra couldn't fathom having those powers, using them to hurt other people ... being evil. She had always embraced the goodness and she always would.

"I've told you. I like my life. *This* is what I want. Not that," she said flipping her hands toward him.

"But I can give you everything! The world!"

Cassandra pressed the palms of her hands against her temples. She inhaled deeply and blew it out slowly. "I've told you, Jordan. I don't want it. You have it. You do what you want with your life and I will pray for you. But please just leave me alone."

"You really want to live like *this*?" Jordan asked, throwing his arm out in a sweeping motion, indicating life in the wilderness. "You really do?"

"Yes. This is my life and I *want* it. I have a daughter I love ... and a husband ..."

Something flickered in Jordan's eyes. "When was the last time you saw your husband?"

"He's been at war."

"And you've heard nothing?"

Cassandra shook her head, studying her brother, hearing something new in his voice. His eyes softened and his whole face seemed to sag with an inexplicable sadness. He averted his eyes and bowed his head. Cassandra's heart stopped.

"What is it?" she whispered.

Jordan didn't answer her, just stared at the ground.

"*What?*" she yelled. "What is it? What do you know?"

"Cassandra." He stopped, as if unable to continue.

A lump bigger than an olive lodged in her throat. Tears sprang to her eyes.

"Tell me," she shouted. "Tell me, Jordan! What do you know?"

"I'm sorry, little sister," he whispered. "I saw him on the battlefield just the other day."

Her heart jumped then began racing with panic. "Where? If I can get to him, I can save—"

Jordan shook his head. "I mean his body. I saw his body. They were burn—"

"No," she yelled, throwing herself at him and pounding her fists against his chest. "You're lying! You just want me to go with you."

He grabbed her shoulders and held her back. "I wish I were. I saw him myself. Here."

He dug in his pouch and handed her a small metal disc with a leather strap laced through a hole in it. She recognized it. She'd found the disc in the dirt their first day out on their own. The leather strap had come from her sandal at the time. She'd made this necklace. She'd given it to Niko.

She stared at the dirt-encrusted disc in her hand and shook her head. Jordan placed his hand on her shoulder, as if to console her. Like she believed he had any grief for her.

"Go away," she said through clenched teeth. "Just leave me alone."

"Cassandra—"

"I mean it, Jordan." Her voice rose higher and louder. "Just leave me alone once and for all. *GET OUT OF MY LIFE!*"

Jordan watched her for another long moment and then disappeared. Finally alone, she gripped the necklace and held her fist against her chest as her heart shattered into a million pieces.

Chapter 12

Jordan held the cup to his mouth and gagged. Eris's potions always smelled as if she'd mixed feces with decomposing body parts, but the blood of the original vampyre must have made this one worse.

"This won't change me, will it?" he asked her. "I don't want to be a vampyre."

The idea of actually becoming a blood-sucker—the vilest creatures of them all—disgusted him.

Eris blew out an exasperated breath. "As I've said countless times, no. There are just a few drops from Zardok. And the blood and venom of the Weres and some of my blood and my magick. Mixed with your own nature, you will have the best qualities of all of us but be none of us."

"Perfect. Just what I need and exactly what Zardok wants."

"Which is the only reason he gave his blood in the first place. He wasn't happy at first about what you tried to pull on him. At least, not until he saw the devastation you caused for your sister."

"He likes his new child."

"Yes, he does. That was very risky, Jordan."

"Risky, yes. But also clever because it obviously worked," he said with a grin. "Will I have that mind connection vampyres have with their victims?"

"He didn't drink *your* blood and I just said, he's not siring you. You might see brief glimpses of his mind, but it shouldn't last."

Jordan shuddered with that thought. "I should hope not. I wouldn't want to know what goes on in that demon's head. Then again . . ." He tapped his finger against the cup's rim. ". . . knowing what he's thinking could be a valuable gift. I suppose it is time to find out."

He lifted the cup in a one-sided toast, brought it to his lips, closed his eyes tightly and drank.

The hot liquid burned down his throat and into his stomach. He choked it all down and the bubbling potion immediately cooled and froze his insides. An icy river surged through his veins and shivers became convulsions. He collapsed, his whole body numbed and his vision blacked out.

His consciousness remained, but he was no longer in his home with Eris and Deimos, but somehow in the Ancients' cavern. His viewpoint was different than usual, however, and he realized he looked out at the room from one of the thrones. He felt Zardok's delight as if it were his own, filling his frozen chest with pride and excitement. *Wonderful,* the vampyre's voice came in his mind. Fleeting images of Zardok's memories flashed before Jordan's eyes then faded to nothing.

He didn't know how long he left his mind for Zardok's, but when he came back to himself, he no longer felt frozen and numb. Rather, he now felt air stirring against his skin and wondered why Eris and Deimos would have carried him outside. He opened his eyes. He still lay on the floor in their house, staring at the ceiling. The air he'd felt moving was only from Eris and Deimos's breathing. His senses had heightened even more. Eris's face came into view, hovering over him, and he almost screamed with fright. What happened to her? She looked even older and uglier than before.

Her mouth pulled into a sad smile, her skin wrinkling more. "It drained me. But I think it worked, Jordan."

He slowly sat up, knowing from previous experiments with the potions that the heightened senses could be overwhelming if he moved too quickly. This time felt different, though. Natural. He thought she was right. It had worked.

"Dagger," he said. Deimos handed him his favorite blade and he pulled the edge across his arm. He growled, a feral, hair-raising sound, even to himself. Although he felt everything else, he felt no pain. But the knife still cut his skin. He threw the dagger across the room and the point stuck into the stone wall, the metal blade twanging with vibration. "I can still be injured. It didn't work!"

The roar made both Deimos and Eris jump several paces backwards.

"Give it time," Eris said. "It takes a new vampyre three days to fully transform. It takes a Were until the full moon. Be patient, Jordan. I know it will work. It *has* to."

Jordan stared at the place where he'd just cut himself. His skin looked perfect, not even a pink line revealing what he'd just done. He had to admit this was progress. And he knew Eris was right. New vampyres could rise the same night of being turned, but they didn't completely change over for three days and it took years for them to master their powers. He'd waited this long. He could wait a little longer. At least he didn't have the uncontrollable urge to drink blood. Another good sign.

"What about you?" he demanded. "You look like a were-boar."

Her eyes flashed with anger, a spark in their cloudiness.

"My father can draw energy from the world. He can replace mine . . . that I sacrificed for *you*."

"He better," Jordan muttered.

Everything took longer than desired. Days turned into weeks, weeks became months and he saw gradual improvements in both him and Eris. He forced himself to have patience, knowing if he gained true immortality, time no longer meant anything. He could even deal with Eris for her short time left in this world. Besides, he still needed her. He wasn't through using her yet. He had more plans.

℘

"Someone is coming," Eris said.

She sat in the grass, watching Jordan teach Deimos how to fight as he prepared their son to become his second-in-command. Jordan followed her gaze into the valley behind their home and paid for the distraction: his son's sword came down on his bare shoulder. He sucked in a breath, but when he looked at where the blade should have sliced through, he saw nothing. No blood. Not so much as a scratch. He grinned at Deimos. *Finally.*

And the next thing he knew, an icy hand clamped around his throat. "You're a monster! Just as you've made me!"

Jordan grabbed the assailant's wrist and twisted his arm, making him release his grasp and cry out in pain. He grinned again. He'd just overpowered a vampyre.

"*I* didn't make you a monster," he said, holding the vampyre at arm's length. "Zardok did."

"You may as well have." He spit in Jordan's face. "You found me. You ordered it. And now I can't go back to my wife and daughter because all I can think about is the taste of their blood!"

Jordan shoved him to the ground and wiped the vampyre

saliva from his cheek. "Pity you haven't killed them yet."

He didn't mean it. He had plans for this vampyre's family. The bloodsucker came at him again in a blur, but Jordan's keen eyesight could track him and he stopped the attack with a flick of his hand.

"You don't want to do that," Jordan said. "You don't want to kill me. I'm the only family you have left. Except for the others like you."

"*Family?*" the man barked.

"We are brothers-in-law, no?"

Niko hissed the way only a vampyre could. Jordan chuckled.

"I have no family, thanks to you. Not those monsters and definitely not you. I'll have nothing to do with any of you!" And with that, Niko disappeared.

Jordan shook his head. As commander of the Daemoni, he should probably track down the vampyre, but he didn't worry about him. How much harm could he cause by himself, especially when he still had a conscience? One of the downfalls of forcing the turns was that the newly changed held onto their humanity, sometimes for years, unlike those given the choice to exchange their souls for immortality. But when on the battlefields, they didn't have time or patience—or desire—to offer that choice. Such as with Niko, who *had* to be turned for the greater good of everyone. And, of course, for the greater good of Jordan. He would give Niko more time to accept what he'd become before bringing him into his army.

"So," Jordan said, looking at Eris and then at Deimos and back at the witch. "The potion worked. Now we move onto the next step."

"Next step?" Eris asked with bewilderment. He hadn't shared this part of his plan with her yet.

"We still have potion left, yes?"

"In a pot sealed with my strongest preservation spell. You said to make enough to share. Who are we sharing it with? It won't affect Daemoni blood."

Jordan looked at his son and grinned. "We start with Deimos."

Deimos' eyes widened. "Why me?"

"Why not?" Jordan asked. "Don't you want this?"

His son scoffed. "I don't need it. I have Mother's blood and yours. I'm already more powerful than you ever were."

In an instant, Jordan had Deimos by the neck, lifted in the air, his legs dangling several feet above the ground.

"Don't be a fool," Jordan growled. "You will take this gift. We haven't worked all this time for you to throw the opportunity away."

Deimos responded only with a blink. Jordan tossed him away. The boy flew back several paces and landed on his back with a hard thud that knocked the wind out of him. He remained motionless, staring at the blue sky.

Jordan turned with disgust and called over his shoulder, "Still think you're more powerful than me?"

Within the hour, Jordan, Eris and Deimos gathered around a cup of brew. A single cup, held in Deimos' shaking hands. Running out of patience, Jordan glanced at the bruises encircling his son's throat and back at his eyes, which filled with more fear. Jordan twitched his hand, about to grab the cup and force Deimos to drink the potion, but then his son lifted the cup to his lips. Jordan pulled in a breath and held it. He watched Deimos force down the entire contents and then collapse in convulsions, just as he had done. He didn't let out his breath for several minutes, not until Deimos finally passed out.

The potion had an immediate effect. Rather than several months, as it had taken Jordan, Deimos changed in weeks. His body grew tall and his muscles developed, transforming him into a full-grown man. Jordan and Eris began to fear their son would never stop aging, that the potion would have the opposite effect of the desired immortality and he would die of old age though he was only a boy. But then the signs of growing older ceased as quickly as they'd started. He appeared to have matured ten years in two weeks, stopping at the prime time of life with a perfect warrior's build. Jordan didn't stop worrying, though, until he felt sure Deimos would never age another day again.

Jordan spent his time overseeing the training of his new army. The battles across Thessaly, Athena and Corinth had ended, leaving them few fallen soldiers to turn. He didn't worry, though. Humans harbored a love affair with war and there would always be another one. In the meantime, they had already doubled their numbers and these new Daemoni needed training. Jordan saw another way to build the army, as well: reproduce more like him and Deimos. But first they needed females for mating.

"It's time to take the potion to Andronika," he announced to Eris one evening.

"Your niece?" she asked with surprise.

"I'd rather my sister, but she's aged too much. Andronika's blood is as close to mine as we can get."

"When do you want to leave?"

"When can you have more potion ready?"

"Give me a moon cycle. But we're running out of Zardok's blood. I only have enough for this one batch. He's been generous, but I doubt he'll give us any more."

Jordan stroked his chin with thought. "It's enough. She's a young girl. She'll only need part of it. If this goes as planned and Zardok sees the potential for our army, he'll gladly give all we want."

❧

Eris swept her hands over her body. "Do I look like the caring type?"

Jordan eyed her. He would have preferred pretty and

youthful Inga to do this task, but they hadn't heard from the witch in years. Not since he'd dismissed her from their home so they could concentrate on the potions. He couldn't deliver the potion himself—Cassandra would never trust him again—so he had no choice but to rely on Eris.

"You still look old," he grumbled.

"Like a grandmotherly type? That's the point. But do I look like a *trustworthy* grandmother? The kind who holds a sick child or teaches her how to cook?"

Jordan shrugged. He had no idea what a caring grandmother looked like, never having had one of his own. "I suppose."

Eris pulled in a deep breath and blew it out. "Then it is time."

She left Jordan in the forest that opened to the cliff where Cassandra and her daughter still resided. They'd been watching the woman and the girl for several days. Cassandra rarely emerged from their cave and when she did, her face was always drawn tight and her eyes filled with pain and sadness. Her hair was usually loose and tangled, streaked with nearly as much gray as Eris's, and she no longer held her head high. She still grieved for her husband, not knowing he wasn't exactly dead . . . but not quite alive, either.

The change in his sister stirred something unfamiliar in Jordan. She used to be so strong, so brave and so determined. He secretly admired her for her courage and unwavering beliefs, even if she believed wrongly. Now she looked lost and defeated. He didn't understand how the loss of a man could break her. He knew he had been responsible for this change in her . . . and he could make it better, too. Perhaps he should have Eris slip her the potion after all. It could give her a better life. *What was that?* Was that foreign feeling *guilt*?

Disgusted with himself, he shook it off, crept to the edge of the tree line and watched as Eris approached Andronika and struck up a conversation. Relief washed over Jordan when the girl smiled. She already trusted Eris, who led her farther away from the shelter where Cassandra remained, pointing out a clump of the plants the girl sought. After a while, they sat for a rest and Eris pulled out the water skins. She offered one to Andronika and Jordan listened with his inhumanly keen hearing.

"I have my own. You save yours," the girl said politely, opening her satchel.

"But does yours heal sadness?" Eris asked, her voice softer and kinder than Jordan had ever heard it.

Andronika's brows furrowed. "No. It's just water. How do you know I'm sad?"

"I can feel it around you. I can see it in your eyes. Here." Eris held the water skin out. "Just try it."

Andronika took the water skin, but didn't immediately drink from it. She held it under her nose and sniffed. Jordan silently congratulated himself for insisting Eris add something to improve the smell and flavor.

"What's in it?" his niece asked.

Eris listed a few herbs that Andronika would know were harmless.

"And it will make the sadness leave?"

"Yes, dear. You will see the world differently. Better."

Andronika hesitated. Jordan's heart pounded against his ribs and his body tensed with the anticipation. If she reacted as Deimos did, soon Andronika would change permanently and be his forever. He would defeat his sister and prove how right he'd always been. He grinned with this thought, glad to be rid of that sickening feeling of guilt. After what felt like fifty moon cycles, Andronika finally drank the potion. Jordan stopped breathing as he and Eris both watched the girl. And waited.

But nothing happened.

Andronika smiled appreciatively at Eris and handed the water skin back to the witch. Then she stood and returned to her gathering. *She should be writhing in pain and collapsing with the effects!* It took every bit of control Jordan possessed to stay behind the trees, out of his niece's sight. Rage built within him, turning his vision red. *What went wrong?* He debated whether to attack the girl first or the witch who had apparently made a mistake. A big mistake. Or had she tried to fool him? His chest heaved. A growl rumbled in his throat. He couldn't stand it a second longer. He wanted to kill the stupid witch.

But just as he thought to make the move, Andronika collapsed.

He and Eris rushed to her side. She lay on the ground, her eyes rolled back in her head. Eris placed her hand over the girl's lids and closed them.

"Is she dead?" Jordan demanded. That would be worse than the potion not working. At least if she were alive, they could try again. He placed his finger against the girl's neck and felt a faint beating. He blew out the breath he'd been holding and rocked back on his heels. "Is it working?"

Eris stared at the girl, not answering at first. She held her hands over the girl's heart and moved them along her body without actually touching her. Then she looked up at Jordan, her dark eyes filled with bewilderment.

"I don't know. I can feel the magick running through her veins, but I can't feel any effects from it." She tapped a finger against her lips. "She's more human than you or Deimos. It might take longer."

"Does she need more potion?"

"More would kill her. Her signs are already faint."

Jordan nodded. They both sat back and waited and watched Andronika sleep. And waited. And watched. As the sun slid across the sky and behind the trees, Jordan grew concerned. If

Andronika didn't return home soon, Cassandra might come looking for her. She couldn't find him here, but they couldn't abandon the unconscious girl, either. Cassandra could mix a concoction to try to revive her daughter and possibly ruin the potion's effects. He opened his mouth to tell Eris they needed to move her, but then the girl's body stirred. Jordan flashed, appearing a hundred paces away, and watched.

Andronika's eyes fluttered open. She looked at Eris at first with confusion and then with recognition. Eris helped her sit up.

"How do you feel?" Eris asked.

The girl seemed to consider the question. "Well, I guess. Not much different, though. Wait . . . I suppose the sadness has lifted. I don't feel so heavy."

"Is that all?"

Andronika rolled her shoulders and stretched her neck. "I feel like I slept for days. How long did I?"

"Just the afternoon."

Andronika looked around. Eris and Jordan both studied her carefully, watching for any indication the girl gave of improved hearing or sight.

"The sky is darkening. I better return to Mother," she said, rising to her feet. "Thank you for sharing your drink. I think it's working."

The girl skipped off and Jordan and Eris just watched, their mouths open. By the time Jordan thought to react, she was already disappearing inside the shelter. An angry roar started building in his core, pushing its way upward. He let it out when Eris appeared by his side. She jumped back several feet.

"Calm down," she snapped.

"Calm down?" Jordan echoed, his voice like ice. He flashed right in front of her and grabbed her by the throat. "Calm *down*? What did you do, woman? You ruined the potion!"

Pain pulsed through Jordan's hand and Eris's spell forced

him to release her. She held a hand up, threatening him.

"Yes, calm down. I could still feel the magick within her. Just give it time."

Jordan snarled at her. "What did you do to the potion? How did you change it?"

"Nothing, except add the lavender and vanilla for flavor. That wouldn't change the effects."

Jordan crossed his arms and narrowed his eyes. "You think it will work?"

"If it doesn't, it's not because of the potion. It's because of the girl. She might be too human."

Jordan rubbed his chin with his thumb and forefinger for a long, silent moment. "Then we wait and we watch. When she starts showing signs, we must get to her before her mother does."

❧

Jordan couldn't wait long. His army needed attention. The new recruits lacked control over their bloodlust and would betray them all if he didn't act. The Daemoni wouldn't have the numbers to overtake humanity for a few human generations, and if they exposed themselves too early, the humans would fight back. He would lose all the progress he'd made. So he left Eris to keep an eye on the girl.

After several weeks, Eris returned, appearing at his side as he watched a pack of werewolves train.

"It's not working," she said, avoiding any preliminaries.

Jordan snarled, the sound muffled by the growling and snapping of teeth from the fight pit. The revelation wasn't a surprise to him—after all this time he'd come to accept the girl's human weakness—but it still angered him to hear it pronounced. He had another plan, though.

"How much potion is left?" he asked.

"Enough for two."

"Take it all and go to Cassandra."

Eris sucked in a breath. "We agreed she might be too old. It could—"

"She's the last chance we have. If it doesn't work, give both her and the girl the rest. Even if it kills them."

At this, a wicked glint shone in Eris's eyes as her lips turned up in a smile. "If that's what you want."

"Yes. That's exactly what I want." Jordan looked back at the fight pit where two wolves tore at each other with long fangs and claws. One of the wolves grabbed the other with its mouth, clamping its teeth on its throat, drawing blood. Excitement surged through Jordan's body. "And I want to watch. Fetch me when you're ready."

Two days later, Jordan crouched in the woods again as Eris greeted Andronika in the field of flowers.

"Hello, again," Andronika said with a smile on her face.

"Hello, sweet one. I see you feel much better."

"I do. Your juice worked!" The girl studied the older woman's face, biting her lower lip, as if wanting to ask something but not having the courage to do it. Then she finally blurt it out. "Do you have any more? I'd like Mother to try it. She really needs it. She's so sad, sadder than even I was, and I've failed to make her better."

Eris smiled and so did Jordan. The girl couldn't have made it any easier.

Andronika ran for the shelter and reappeared a few minutes later, tugging on her mother's hand. Cassandra stumbled after her daughter, blinking against the brightness of the morning sun. She looked even worse than she had before, her face vacant, her eyes distant, as if she didn't see anything in this place or time. As if she was lost in the past. He recognized the look—

their Father had carried it for some time after Mother had died.

"Here, Mother," Andronika said, placing Eris's water skin in her mother's hand. "This is what made me better. It will make you better, too."

Although the change in Jordan allowed his mind to run several thoughts at once, he focused every bit of himself on his sister. He watched her eyes travel to the water skin in her hand and back to her daughter, as if not comprehending. His pulse raced as Andronika forced her mother's hand up, lifting the skin to her lips. His breath caught as she drank without question. And his heart leapt.

He'd finally done it. His twin sister would have to see his side now. She would have to believe him now. She would have to admit he'd been right all along. She would *have* to join the Daemoni, where she belonged.

Chapter 13

A voice in the back of Cassandra's mind told her not to drink from the water skin, that something was amiss about this grandmotherly woman and the drink she offered. The back of her neck tingled with the feeling of being watched and not just by Andronika and this woman. Her daughter's eyes looked so hopeful, however, and she'd witnessed a definitive change in Andronika. Her mood had brightened and she just seemed more alive than either of them had since learning of Niko's death.

Andronika had attempted to reproduce the concoction on her own, saying the woman had told her the herbal ingredients, but she'd never been able to replicate it—nothing she made had the same effects. Cassandra could smell the same ingredients Andronika used in the water skin now, but she also smelled a bitter tang underneath the lavender, vanilla and other herbs. Perhaps that was the missing ingredient she needed. Or perhaps she was making a big mistake. But she didn't want to disappoint her daughter and, by now, she was willing to do anything to move beyond her grief for Niko. So when Andronika lifted the skin to her mouth, she drank.

The liquid felt neither warm nor cool in her mouth, but as soon as it hit the pit of her belly, it seemed to freeze. A bitter cold spread among her insides and her stomach tightened painfully, making her cry out. Icy shards entered her bloodstream and traveled throughout her body. Her heart sped, as if trying to outrun the cold, and uncontrollable shivers wracked her shoulders and arms. Her teeth slammed against each other and she tried to wrap her arms around herself, but she couldn't make them move. She'd never been so cold in her life, even when she'd bathed in the streams up north during the winter.

"Mother," Andronika shrieked with alarm. "What's wrong with her?"

Cassandra never heard the answer. The shivers became more violent, more like the convulsions soldiers suffered just before dying. Unable to control herself or to feel any part of her body, she collapsed. She struggled to breathe, but she couldn't draw in even the slightest bit of air and what was left in her lungs felt heavy and frozen. She wanted to say good-bye to her daughter, but couldn't. Her head felt as though she'd been plunged into icy water and the words remained frozen in her mind. Her heart silenced. Everything went numb. The world disappeared.

Cassandra's mind floated in a sea of blackness that became a gray fogginess and when the fog began to clear, a strangled scream caught in her throat. *I've been a good person. I led a good life. Why am I here?* The scene in front of her, surrounding her, had to be Hell. Strangely colored fires blossomed around a dark, round cavern. Cloaked figures sat next to her on thrones that circled the room. Pure evil filled the air, a tangible feeling that wrapped tightly around her, trying to suffocate her. *If I'm here . . . then Jordan was right . . . we are demons.*

"*Yes, Jordan was right,*" a terrifying voice echoed in her mind. "*He was also right about you. You are stronger than we expected. You are a nice addition to the Daemoni.*"

The Daemoni? The word rang with familiarity, something Jordan must have told her.

New visions flashed in her mind. Men and women waving their hands and sparks of light emitting from them, causing trees to burst into flames and water to rise out of lakes. Then she saw others, their bodies shimmering and then exploding. They disappeared, replaced by fierce beasts—some familiar, some she'd never seen before, all growling and snarling. More images showed men and women with white skin and perfect features except for their red eyes and teeth that looked like animal fangs. She watched in horror as those fangs slashed into the throats of innocent people, the monsters reveling in the taste of the blood.

Then she saw Niko, her own dear, sweet husband, and tears sprang to her eyes. He, too, had the same pale skin . . . and fangs dripping crimson. His tongue ran over the tip of one fang, savoring the blood, his eyes closed and he grinned, as if he were in Heaven. But this was not Heaven.

"*No, it is not. But it's not Hell, either,*" said the frightening voice. "*We are the Daemoni. We've brought Hell to Earth. And you will help us rule.*"

Never! She wanted to cry out.

"*It is time you accepted who—what—you really are. Jordan has given you new powers—*"

Jordan? He did this to me? She heard her brother's laugh in her mind, drowning out the other one.

"*Yes, little sister. I've made you like me. Together, we can rule the Daemoni. Rule the world.*"

She remembered the powers he'd displayed the last time she'd seen him and her frozen heart contracted, shooting pain through her chest.

I don't want to be like you. I told you that. I don't want these powers. How could you do this to me?

"*It's too late to fight it. Accept it. Embrace it. We will dominate! Earth will belong to the Daemoni and Satan will finally rule. Because of us.*"

"*No!*" The new voice bellowed from what sounded like right in her ear but also far away.

Cassandra looked up and through a shimmering haze, she saw Father, with his large, white wings and long blades in each hand. But he wasn't alone. The creature he battled also had wings, but black and rather than covered in feathers, a thin membrane stretched across them, like a bat's wings. Horns protruded from its head and its eyes glowed red. It swung a black, jagged blade at Father, but he blocked it with one sword and jabbed at the demon with the other. The clash of metal against metal pierced Cassandra's ears. The demon's tail whipped, its pointed end slashing at Father, but missing. Father and the demon flew and twisted and rolled in the air, their blades arcing and slicing and parrying each other's blows. Cassandra gasped when Father lost one of his blades.

"*You have to choose, my daughter,*" Father spoke in her head. "*Choose the life you want. The God you follow.*"

I've always chosen our life. Our God. The One and Only.

Father gripped his remaining sword in both hands, spun in the air and arced it down, slicing through the demon's throat. The head fell from the body. Black blood spurted. A hundred voices screamed in Cassandra's ears, denying the loss.

"*Then your soul is ours, my daughter. It always will be.*"

Father lifted her in his strong arms and warmth flooded back into her body. Her heart restarted and the heat built inside her and spread throughout, down her arms and legs and into her fingers and toes. Her skin tingled as she regained feeling.

Then the heat became too much and she writhed in her father's arms, screaming at him to douse the fire. Liquid flames licked through her veins. And then her vision grayed out again.

When it returned, she was back on the cliff top and she blinked against the bright light. Several paces away, Andronika and the old woman stared down at a body. Her body. *How could that be?* And there, on the edge of the cliff, stood a familiar figure. His wings were closed against his back. He turned when he sensed her.

"Are we on Earth or in Heaven?" Cassandra asked him, confused by seeing her deathly still body separate from herself, her soul. He appeared suddenly right in front of her and reached his hand out to touch her face. She nuzzled her cheek against his palm. His blue eyes filled with love and longing.

"In between," he said. "We're on the edge of the Otherworld, at the veil."

She remembered the veil from when he'd shared visions of his past before leaving them on Earth. She wasn't exactly dead, but— *Oh, no! Andronika!* Her hand flew to her throat. Father took it between his.

"You *will* return to the Earthly realm," he said. "Your time there is not nearly over."

She let out a sigh of relief, tainted with grief. "I've missed you, Father."

"I've been here all along. Just on the other side of the veil."

"What's happened to me? What did Jordan do?" Her voice rose several octaves as terror overcame her. "Will I be like *him* now?"

Why didn't he just kill her? She'd rather be dead than be evil.

"Yes and no," Father said. "Those visions you saw before were images of the Daemoni—mages, vampyres, were-animals—beasts created by the demons as Satan's army."

"Jordan's told me about them." Her words felt heavy, her voice thick. She refused to be a part of them.

"Jordan has given you a potion that combines their qualities."

Cassandra choked on the breath that lodged in her throat. Father wrapped his arms around her.

"Do not worry. All will be well," he said.

"How can you say that? I don't want to be like him! How can this happen? Couldn't you have prevented it?"

"We allowed it."

Cassandra pushed back from Father's embrace and gaped at him.

"You allowed him to turn me into a . . . a *monster?*"

"We allowed him to create the potion. We allowed him to give it to you. That's been his purpose all along. But this is actually our gift to you, so you may serve *your* purpose."

"*My* purpose?" Her eyes flashed. "And what would that be? Hurting and killing innocent people? Because that seems to be all they do!"

"That's what *they* do. Not you." He took her hand again. "Come for a walk with me and let me explain. We have important plans for you and your descendants and I only have a short time to tell you everything before sending you back."

Cassandra walked with her father along the cliff's edge, the waves crashing against the rocks below them and sending up a spray that she could see but not feel. Although this was her and Andronika's cliff that had become so familiar to her, it felt different—not quite real. She couldn't deny her father's request to clarify even if she wanted to, because she had no idea how to return to her own realm.

Father explained how the fallen angels—the demons—created the Daemoni and how the Daemoni were now building their army by infecting and turning innocent humans. He told her how they did this to Niko. She shook her head, denying that her husband could be like them. But then she remembered the vision she'd seen, what Father explained was a memory being shared with her by a vampyre named Zardok.

"Can I do anything for him?" she asked. "He can't *want* to be with them."

To her surprise, Father smiled down at her. "That's exactly what your purpose is. No, Niko does not want to be with them. Neither do many of those they've turned. We allowed the creation of this potion, knowing Jordan would give it to you. We saw an opportunity for the Angels to build our own army on Earth, which is why we allowed it." Father's wings lifted slightly from his back. "The Daemoni need to be countered. They must be kept in check. Yes, you *can* do something."

"But what? How? I'm just like him now!"

"You are not. Through this, we have given you our own gifts. Gifts of the Angels. You will use these gifts to convert those Daemoni souls that can still be saved. Some are already damned and you won't be able to help them. But most retain some level of humanity and there is still hope for them. You can teach them how to live a good life, how to overcome their innate desires for human blood and flesh, how to use their magick for good, rather than evil."

"They will want this?"

"Some will. Others will take convincing. Sometimes you may have to fight."

"Fight?" Cassandra shook her head. "I can't do that, Father."

"You must, my daughter. Just as you saw me fighting that demon, this is a battle you must partake in. You are fighting for God and fighting for souls. If there is ever any reason to raise a sword against another, this is it."

"I don't even know how to fight, though."

"Oh, but you do. We have given you powers, some to help people and others to aid you in battle." He reached behind his shoulder and drew out a dagger from a sheath strapped to his back. "I made this for you. The vampyres will be the hardest to kill. The Daemoni believe only vampyres can slay other vampyres, but we have provided another weapon to be used against them and all the Daemoni. Silver. Like this blade."

She stared at the weapon he held out to her, not wanting to take it. A large, purple stone was embedded into the silver and gold pattern surrounding the hilt. It was a beautiful piece of art. She shook her head again.

"I can't . . . *kill*."

"You must protect yourself and your people, Cassandra. You must protect those who cannot protect themselves. Even if it means killing Daemoni."

Father pressed the hilt against her palm and closed her fingers around it. The hilt warmed in her hand and the feeling spread upward into her arm. Now that she held it, she couldn't bring herself to let go. She swung it as she'd seen Niko do while practicing his skills and the feeling felt just as natural as scratching an itch.

She blew out a breath of resignation. "And I must do this alone?"

"We will be behind you all the time, just across the veil, helping when you need it. You will grow your army, though, with those who convert. They will come to your side and fight for you against the Daemoni. You will lead them and later, Andronika will take over."

Cassandra's breath caught. "Andronika? Oh, no, Father! Please don't bring her into this. She doesn't—"

"It is too late. She already drank the potion, remember?"

"But nothing happened to her."

"Yet. We have infused the powers of the potion into her blood and bone so that she may pass the qualities on to her children. Then, when it is time, she will change, too. She will receive our gifts, gain her powers and eventually, lead the army you are creating. She will grow it even more and pass it on to her own daughter. Your female descendants will lead this army for as long as they continue to exist on Earth . . . or as long as the Daemoni exists."

They walked in silence for several long moments and the more Cassandra thought about what Father had told her, the more she realized what a daunting task the Angels had given her. Why her? How would she ever be able to do this? Hundreds of questions flew through her mind but only one managed to come out of her mouth.

"How do I save their souls?"

"Lead them to the decision to desire it. Share your goodness with them and convince them to change. We will show the way from there."

Before she could ask another question, Father suddenly stopped and whipped around.

"Our time is over," he said. "Andronika needs us."

He nodded to the place where they had started, where Cassandra had drunk the potion in the Earthly realm. Through the shimmery air of the veil, Cassandra saw her daughter and the old woman arguing. Her breath caught as the woman grabbed Andronika in a tight hold. Her daughter thrashed her arms and legs but the woman held her tightly with unnatural strength.

"Andronika!"

Another figure—a very familiar one—darted out of the woods. *Oh, no!*

"Go, Cassandra," Father ordered. "Cross through the veil and help her. Then help Niko. He needs you. I'll be fighting from here."

An ear-piercing screech cut through the air and two demons,

blades drawn, flew at them. Cassandra couldn't move, her heart torn. She couldn't leave her father to fight these terrible beasts.

"I can handle this. You must do your part. This is your purpose, Cassandra. Go! They need you!"

Those last three words were what she needed to hear to get her moving. Her heart already pounding in her chest, she sprinted across the field, fighting the urge to look back.

"*Don't worry about me,*" Father's voice said in her head. "*I can't be killed. But the ones I protect need to win their fights in the Earthly realm to survive. Save them, Cassandra. We've given you everything you need. Go!*"

The clang of metal against metal and a demonic roar rang in her ears as she crossed through the veil and her spirit slammed into her physical body. She gazed over at where she had left Father, only to see blue sky and the field atop the cliff. He and the demons were invisible to her now.

A scream from her other side jerked her into complete consciousness. She sprang to her feet faster than humanly possible and the movement surprised her. In front of her, though, Andronika still fought the witch's hold and Niko crouched, his muscles taut and fangs bared, ready to charge. Something fell from Cassandra's hand and landed with a thud at her feet, but she couldn't pull her eyes away from the scene to see what it was. She didn't have time to wonder about herself or everything Father had just told her. Her family needed her.

Chapter 14

Is she dead? From his vantage point, Jordan couldn't tell if the potion had killed his sister. She didn't move. She didn't appear to be breathing. Something slammed into his chest, as if someone heaved a large boulder at him, taking his breath away. But nothing was there. Nothing physical. *Another useless emotion.* How weak of him, to feel grief at the loss of a woman who did nothing but annoy him. Maybe that wasn't the loss he felt, though. Maybe it was the loss of what he'd had planned. Yes, that made more sense.

At least he still had Andronika. He twitched his finger and the girl flew into Eris's arms. The witch held her tightly.

And then Cassandra moved.

"Stop," she yelled, suddenly on her feet. "Release my daughter."

Eris's mouth fell open with initial shock, but she recovered quickly. Her eyes narrowed and one of her fingers just barely flicked—not enough to lose her grip on Andronika, but enough to send a flash of light at Cassandra, who threw her hand up to block it. Not only did the spell ricochet off her hand and over the cliff, but Eris's arms were forced free from Andronika and the witch flew backwards several paces. She slammed against a tree trunk and landed on her backside. Again she gaped. Then she disappeared.

Jordan chuckled. *Nice work, little sister.*

"*Jordan?*" she answered in his mind. He started with the shock of it. "*You can enter my mind? Is this another of your powers?*"

Ah, you can hear me and I can hear you. No, I only wish I had such an ability. It's not my power doing this.

"*I don't understand.*"

You're doing this, little sister. Welcome to my world.

He heard her growl in his mind and then with his ears.

"Leave us alone, Jordan," she yelled at him aloud. "I will *not* be like you."

Accurately sensing him, she threw her hands in his direction, as if shooing him away. A strong wind erupted from where she stood and blew into the woods. Her familiar scent filled his senses and he nearly retched—she smelled more disgustingly sweet than she ever had. He couldn't believe how strong her powers were.

And he couldn't believe she was still *good*.

Amazement and agitation coursed through his veins and he flashed back home. Eris stood in the center of the room, her eyes glazed over and her mouth still open.

"What happened?" Jordan demanded.

Eris's mouth shut, then opened and shut again, words failing her. Her eyes remained distant.

"She's so . . . so beautiful," the witch stammered. "And so *powerful*."

"Something went wrong," Jordan growled. "She's still *good*. I could feel it like a nasty slime in the air and on my skin. This wasn't supposed to happen! How am I supposed to create more like us if I can't even get close to her without retching?"

Eris's eyes finally focused and shot to him. "What do you mean?"

"Building our army, Eris. Reproducing more of us. What else would I want her for?"

Her mouth dropped open again. Her nose pulled up in disgust. "*That's* why you wanted her to drink the potion? So you could *mate* with her? Your *sister?*"

Rage exploded in Jordan's chest at the look Eris gave him. Who was she to judge him? His pulse thundered in his head. He fought the urge to grab her by the neck and strangle her.

"Of course, you doltish witch. Deimos and I need the best mates we can get."

He shot his hand up and the door exploded out of the way. He marched outside, kicked a stone and slammed his fist into the trunk of a cypress, leaving a large dent. A stray dog scampered across the way, whimpering, and Jordan threw a ball of fire at the useless creature. An old woman cried out and he turned his hand toward her. Her eyes widened and she hurried out of his sight.

The old hag's fear made him feel somewhat better, calm enough to try to think through what went wrong with Cassandra. She'd reacted to the potion immediately, even faster than Deimos had. She appeared to age backward many years, back to how she looked several decades ago, like a young woman. And her powers. Were they stronger than his? *Impossible!* But he could definitely feel they were different. He didn't know if he'd ever be able to overcome that difference. *Perhaps it will take time for the Daemoni blood to seep into her core.*

This thought instantly changed his outlook. Of course that was it! He'd need to give it time, just like his transformation took months to gain the full effects. With a sense of relief, he returned to the house. And found Eris in a convulsive fit.

Her eyes rolled back in her head, showing only whites. Her face twisted and contorted, her features growing and shrinking right in front of his eyes. Her body trembled and quaked. Her arms whipped in the air. An object flew out of her hand and landed at his feet. He picked up the water skin and held it under his nose.

"Eris," he bellowed. "What have you done?"

She looked as though she tried to answer, but her enlarged tongue flopped out of her mouth, reminding him of a dead donkey. One of her dark eyes grew larger and larger, until it bulged out of its socket. An arm shrunk in girth to the size of a stick and lengthened to the floor while the other forearm blossomed to twice its normal roundness. Her legs swelled to look like tree trunks. She fell to the floor and writhed and Jordan just watched with fascinated horror.

As the convulsions slowed into shudders and then just tremors, her body began returning to normal. Then it went further back, back in time, just as Cassandra's had done. When she finally stilled, she looked just like the goddess Jordan had first met. He fell to his knees next to her and lifted her head into his lap.

"What have you done?" he asked again, this time his voice filled with awe and wonder rather than surprised anger.

She opened her eyes and smiled. "You wanted a mate like you. You don't need her. You have me and we can have more children together."

"You drank the last of the potion?"

"We can make more. We can build your army, Jordan. Together."

He looked into those beautiful dark eyes and ran his hand through the silky raven hair he missed so much. He didn't think the potion would have worked on her. Eris herself had said Daemoni blood probably wouldn't take it. Not with the other creatures' bloods mixed in it. But here she was, having gone through the same changes as Cassandra, but without that vile goodness surrounding her. He grinned back at her and excitement flooded his veins. Eris was even better than Cassandra. Victory was finally his!

But when he pulled his hand out of her locks, clumps of hair clung to his fingers. He stared at it with surprise and then flicked it off. He looked back at her face and bluish-black marks encircled her eyes and then they began sinking downward. Her luscious lips looked as though they were sliding right off her face. The skin around one sunken eye pulled down. She lifted a skinny, bony hand to rub it and peeled the skin right off, exposing soft, black tissue underneath. Her expression tried to twist in anger, but it only made her face worse.

"*No,*" she screeched. "This cannot be happening!"

She flicked her hand to deliver a spell, but it only resulted in skin flying off her fingers, exposing the bones. Jordan jumped up and her head slammed against the ground. The rest of her hair fell out and her nose crumbled into powder.

"Why?" she shrieked with an inhuman voice, her lips and cheeks peeling away so he could see her tongue moving between her teeth. "Why does she get it all when it was I who sacrificed everything for you?" Her eyeballs rotated in their sockets to look at Jordan. "I'll give you what she never will, Jordan. And then you'll know who truly loved you."

Her mouth moved with unintelligible words that sounded to him like a curse. But he would never know who or what she cursed, because Eris was no more. Everything soft about her shriveled like a dried up plum and then disappeared, leaving only a skull and bones. And then those disintegrated into nothingness. Not even dust remained.

Jordan stared at the spot, his heart pounding and his hands shaking at his side. He drew in a deep breath, but it didn't help. He retched all over the white peplos—all that remained of the woman he'd called his wife, the mother of his son. The only woman who'd stayed by his side all these years, helping him achieve his destiny. The woman who'd thought of him and his needs and wants to the very end. And now she was gone. The freedom he expected to feel when he finally rid himself of Eris didn't come. Only the astonishing feeling of profound emptiness.

Chapter 15

Cassandra no longer felt Jordan's presence. She stared at her hands with wonder. *What gifts have the Angels given me?*

Andronika's whimper caught her attention and she spun around. Her daughter was still on all fours after falling from the witch's hold, staring up at the new threat in front of her. Niko stood tensed for a fight, but his eyes were focused on Andronika and they glowed a bright red. Cassandra's knees weakened to see her husband standing there after mourning for him so long, looking even more striking than she remembered him, but her heart contracted at the frightening look on his face and the feel of his bloodlust surging through his veins.

"*I need it,*" Niko's voice hissed in Cassandra's mind, making her jump. "*I'm already weak from the sun. I need blood.*"

Did she really just hear his thoughts or did her own mind create the illusion?

"F-f-father?" Andronika asked, her voice small and frightened. "Wh-what happened to you?"

"*I need it,*" his voice came again, rough, like a growl. Then it changed, more like the voice she remembered, as he internally fought himself. He shook his head, denying his need. "*But not her. Not my daughter.*"

"No, Niko," Cassandra said. "Not your daughter."

He turned his red-eyed glare on her now. His internal fight played out on his face, his eyes flickering with mixed emotions of love, pain and desire. Desire for her blood.

"*Not you either. I love you.*"

Again, she didn't know if she actually heard him—she'd already heard so many other voices in her head—or if she thought what she wanted to hear, what she wanted him to say aloud. She had to take the chance he'd really thought those three words, though, because he needed love to overcome what had been done to him. If he still felt love, she could help him, just as Father had explained.

"I love you, too," she said and his eyes widened with surprise, acknowledging that she had indeed heard his thoughts. "I can help you, if you want me to. You don't have to be like them. We can even be together again."

He shook his head and his face twisted. "I can't, my love. Look at me. I'm a monster."

She held her hands out to him. "You don't have to be. Let me help you, Niko. Let me show you the way."

She took a step toward him and he didn't disappear or run away or lash out at her. So she took another step and another, until she came within arm's reach. She took his hands into hers, internally cringing at the cold and evil lurking just beneath the surface but externally showing him only love and kindness. Somehow, she knew what to do.

"Andronika, go back to the cave," she said without breaking eye contact with Niko.

"What's wrong with him? Is he ill?"

"Yes, but nothing you can help with. I just need you to go. *Now.*"

Andronika snapped her head at her, not used to her mother's sharp commands. Her mouth fell open.

"What happened to *you?*" her daughter demanded. "You look . . . different."

Cassandra had no idea what Andronika meant and she didn't have time to find out. Niko was her first priority. She couldn't stand the thought of losing him again, especially to such evil.

"We'll talk later, but you need to go."

A low growl rumbled in Niko's throat as a part of him tried to fight Cassandra's touch and the other part fought back the desire to hurt them. She wasn't sure if what she was about to try would work, despite what Father had told her. She didn't want Andronika around in case it didn't.

"But—"

"Go, Andronika!"

Their daughter hesitated only another moment and then sprang to her feet and ran for their shelter. As soon as she was out of sight, Cassandra refocused all her efforts on Niko. She gathered all the goodness within her and pushed it down her arms, through her hands and into him. He screamed as if in pain and tried to jerk free from her grasp, but she wouldn't let go. She just kept pushing the strange energy she'd felt in her body ever since re-entering the physical realm. The power of a good heart and a loving soul, intensified by the Angels. One of the gifts they'd given her. She knew this instinctively.

Niko finally stopped screaming but his body convulsed, causing their arms to whip painfully. Cassandra yanked him closer, wrapped her arms tightly around him to control the seizure and continued pushing the good force into him. Eventually, the convulsions weakened into shudders and then he collapsed against her. She lowered his unconscious body to the ground and sat cross-legged with his head in her lap and one of her hands held firmly against his chest, over his heart, still sharing her power with him. She prayed for him and herself.

"*You're doing perfectly,*" Father whispered in her mind. "*We're winning.*"

With this reassurance, she sat with determination, feeding her love's soul and wondering how on earth she would feed his body when he awoke. She understood he needed blood for energy, but Father had said the vampyres must overcome their thirst for human blood. But how?

As the afternoon sun passed overhead, exhaustion overcame Cassandra. She'd been pushing all her force into Niko until she felt like she had none left. She slumped over on the ground, his head still in her lap, and fell asleep. His stirring awoke her at dark and she bolted upright, feeling renewed and refreshed and glad she didn't dream about all that happened this morning. She didn't want to think about it yet. She just wanted her husband to be well. To be hers again.

Niko opened his eyes and looked up at her. They no longer glowed red, but weren't their beautiful olive-green either. Not quite. But she could see the green there, underneath, like the sun behind a gauzy strip of red clouds. He gave her a weak smile and opened his mouth to talk. She shook her head, already knowing his first thought.

I *love you, too, Niko*, she told him with her mind.

His eyes widened slightly. "*Thirsty. So thirsty.*"

Her heart squeezed, feeling the burn in his throat. As his pain grew into agony and she felt his energy weaken, she could think of only one solution. She held her wrist to his mouth.

"Drink, Niko."

He jerked his head away with more strength than she thought he had. "No. Not from you. I won't hurt you. I won't hurt anyone again."

"You *must*, Niko."

"I would rather die than . . . than to bite you."

"Please, don't say that. You don't know what I've gone through since I thought you were dead. I can help you with this, we'll get you through this, but right now, I don't know what else to do. You must drink."

He pursed his lips tightly shut and shook his head in her lap. His eyes fluttered closed and she felt him weakening even more. Her brave, strong Niko, so weak and powerless. She blew out a sigh of exasperation. *Had he always been so stubborn, too?* She pressed her fingernail against the skin over the blue lines on her wrist and dug in, trying to open a wound. But her fingernail couldn't break the skin. It wouldn't even scratch it. Was this another gift? Impenetrable skin? She might have found it a nice gift from the Angels if it didn't mean she was losing the love of her life. Again.

She glanced around and the moonlight glinted off something shining several paces away. Her breath caught. Father's dagger that she'd dropped upon entering the physical realm. Although it was out of reach, she lifted her hand toward it, willing it to her. She gasped as the dagger lifted off the ground, flew through the air and landed right into her palm. If the silver blade could harm vampyres, surely it could cut her skin. She ran the edge over her wrist and blood flowed freely.

She held her arm over Niko's mouth, forcing him to take her blood. He shook his head, fighting it, and she held him still with her free hand.

"Stop, Niko. You're just making a mess."

He tried to push her arm away but she kept it tight against his mouth. Then, something changed in him and he grabbed onto her arm, pulling it to him instead of pushing. He sucked heartily and with each swallow, she felt his energy strengthen. Eventually, instead of forcing him to drink, she had to force him to stop.

"I'm sorry," he said, wiping his mouth. "But you taste delightful."

Cassandra didn't know whether to laugh or cry. Before she could do anything, he pulled her head down to his and delivered her a kiss that was so deep, so sensuous, so loving, it could almost make up for all the kisses they'd missed since he'd left. She didn't remember his lips feeling so soft but firm, his mouth tasting so deliciously sweet, his touch delivering such heat. He'd always excited her easily, but now the feelings were multiplied a thousand times. Tears streamed down her face as they continued kissing.

"I can't believe you're truly here," she said when they finally broke apart for a breath. "Alive. In my arms again."

His lips turned into a sad smile. "Not exactly alive. Definitely not the same."

She nodded and returned his smile. "I know. Father has told me everything."

His brow furrowed for a moment and then the smile deepened, reaching his eyes. "You were right about God. I was wrong, about Zeus and the others. I learned the hard way, seeing real demons with my own eyes." Then he frowned and sadness filled his face again. "But there is another . . . they called him their lord ... they say my soul is his. I am damned to Hades . . . I mean, to Hell."

Cassandra shook her head. "No, Niko. Father has told me everything. You can still be good. You can still go to Heaven. You just have to choose."

She told him the whole story, from Jordan and Eris's potion to her visit with Father the Angel to leading him back to goodness. Sharing it with him helped her own mind to accept it all, although her heart and soul had affirmed it the moment she saw her husband again and wanted nothing but to save him. She had become something more than human, but it was good. And she had a purpose to fulfill.

"There are others like me—changed against their will," Niko said. "If what you say is true . . . you can help them?"

"Just as I have with you. I suppose that is what I am meant to do. Why I am on this Earth."

She let out a sigh mixed with resignation and frustration. Although she had accepted it completely, she still didn't know how she would accomplish this task she'd been given.

Chapter 16

Jordan leaned his elbows on the thick slab of stone they used as a table and pressed his forehead against his hands. His nostrils flared as he breathed deeply, trying to control his temper.

"She didn't give either of you the spell?" he asked through clenched teeth.

Neither Deimos nor Inga answered him at first.

His son had avoided him for weeks, blaming him for the death of Eris. Jordan vaguely remembered what it was like to lose a mother, but he thought his son was beyond those weak emotions. Because he wasn't, Jordan wanted little do with him right now. He'd been sickened and frustrated with his own grief for Eris; he didn't need another reminder staring him in the face.

Inga had come back just this morning, responding immediately to his summons.

"I hadn't talked to her for years," she finally said. "You both kept me out of this, remember? You said my magick wasn't good enough for you."

Jordan responded with a snarl. "I thought you at least knew something. Had some kind of value."

Inga's only answer was a pout.

"She refused to tell me everything," Deimos said. "I know all but one ingredient and I don't know the incantation. But Father, you really do need to go. You've ignored the Ancients' summons long enough."

"I know!" Jordan growled. He slammed his fist onto the table, cracking the stone in half and making Inga yelp.

He'd avoided answering the Ancients for two days, which was two days too long. The pain in his gut from the magickal pull had become relentless. When he answered their summons, though, he wanted to be able to request more blood from Zardok. But if the old vampyre knew they couldn't recreate the potion, he'd never give it. He was running out of time. If he waited much longer, the agony would overcome even him.

Jordan felt a small hand on his shoulder. He looked over at Inga who looked back at him with wide blue eyes.

"What?" he demanded.

"Let me take care of you before you go," she said. With a snort of disgust, or perhaps jealousy, Deimos left the house.

The thought of bedding Inga was enticing—she'd yet to lose her youthful looks and sumptuous body—but Jordan didn't want everything that came with it.

"Why'd you even come here?" he asked. "You knew what I wanted and you didn't have it. Why are you bothering me?"

She blinked and he watched as her throat worked to swallow.

"With Eris gone . . ." she started and stammered. "I mean . . . I thought . . . I love you, Jordan. I just want to be with you. That's all I ever wanted."

Exactly what he didn't want. Love. What a deception. Nobody truly loved. It was just a bothersome word, full of dishonesty that often fooled the one using the word as much as the one hearing it. It destroyed more often than not, wreaking havoc on people's lives. He wondered if His Lord had created this word.

Inga pushed her hand across his back and to his other shoulder and wrapped her other arm across his front, embracing him. She leaned in to press her lips against his cheek, a soft touch of tenderness, not passion. Part of him ached for her, the part that felt her soft breasts rubbing against his bicep. *No, not her.* He craved almost any woman at this point. But definitely not her and all she would expect from him. He shoved her aside, so hard she fell to the floor.

She looked up at him, her eyes watery and pleading. "I will do anything for you, Jordan. There are many ways I can help you. Whatever you need. Whenever you need it. I may not be as magickally powerful as Eris, but—"

"Exactly. I have no need for you. Be gone, woman!"

She flinched and her lower lip trembled. He thought he would hit her if she cried, but she disappeared just as the first tear fell. With an angry exhale, Jordan pulled himself together before flashing north.

ᕫ

Jordan entered the dark, fire-lit room, prepared with an argument for Zardok. He wasn't prepared, however, for the number of people in the circular cavern—every throne was filled and more stood by the fires. One of the cloaked figures rose from a throne and dropped his hood. Eris's father. Jordan sucked his breath. He'd forgotten about him.

"Did she tell *you* the incantation?" Jordan blurted, too excited to control himself. Surely she'd shared it with her father and the sorcerer was powerful enough to make it work . . . unless, for some reason, he mourned his daughter's death. Jordan didn't think it possible, but he'd stopped trying to figure out the Ancients a long time ago.

"Of course not," the sorcerer sneered. "She was smart enough to know sharing it would make her dispensable. Unfortunately, she wasn't smart enough to overcome her own vanity. Stupid woman, drinking what she knew would poison her."

"Do you plan to help me recreate it?" Jordan asked.

"We already have our best witches working on it."

Jordan's eyes widened and his nostrils flared. He didn't like the idea of others working on *his* potion.

"You, Jordan, have more important things to worry about," Zardok said from his throne. He rose, pushing the naked brunette off his lap and wiping his mouth with his thumb and forefinger. She slipped into the shadows and a dark shape licked the blood trickling down her breast. "Your sister."

Jordan's eyes snapped back to Zardok. "Yes. I thought I would give her time, let the potion take full effect, then retrieve her."

The vampyre chuckled. "Retrieve her? I do not think you understand the gravity of the situation."

"You won't be able to retrieve her," the sorcerer said. "She will never be ours. The Angels have permanently tainted her."

Jordan pressed his lips together. He'd come to realize this already, but he'd been holding onto the hope that the Daemoni qualities would overpower whatever the Angels did to her.

"They have claimed her and her descendants," Zardok added. "And now we have a problem. It's a small one right now, but if you don't do something about it, it will grow. And it's *your* problem, Jordan."

Jordan peered at him and lifted an eyebrow in question.

"We are losing our own to her," Zardok said.

Growls and hisses sounded around the room. Jordan's eyes darted to Zardok's face.

"She's converting your new troops. She's taken Niko back. He's brought her more. We're losing their *souls*, Jordan," Zardok said. "You must stop her."

Anger welled in Jordan's chest, but he just nodded. "I can take care of it. I just need a couple of men."

"You can choose the men you take, except for Deimos," the sorcerer said. "If you fail, we'll still have him."

"I won't fail."

"You should hope not," Zardok said. "Because if she and hers don't kill you, we will."

"I said I can take care of it," Jordan growled. "She's just my sister. I am still far more powerful than she is."

"So be it," Zardok said. "Take care of it. Even if it means killing her."

"Of course," Jordan said with a slight bow to the Ancients.

He had no problem making the promise—he secretly clutched to the hope that his sister could still be useful to him, but if not, and if she was any threat to his future, he would kill her. How, he wasn't sure. After all, his main intent with the potion was immortality. He just hoped that part hadn't taken effect in her yet.

First, he had to find her. Which became more difficult than he expected.

Chapter 17

Cassandra sat on a dead log with her elbows on her knees and her head in her hands. She peeked to her side to ensure Andronika still slept, even with everyone's voices growing louder. She now had six others in the little group Father had told her to create—Niko, two other vampyres, two werewolves and a witch who had just joined them about a month ago. Definitely not an army. Even if she converted a hundred more, she wanted to avoid fighting the Daemoni at all costs. She couldn't put her growing family—she loved them nearly as much as she loved her daughter—at risk. Unfortunately, that's exactly what they wanted to do.

"We've been running from your brother for nearly two seasons," Niko said. "We have more numbers now and we're all trained warriors. We can fight them, Cassandra."

"I don't *want* to fight them," she said for the fifth time tonight.

He'd been making this same plea to her for a while now. Being on the run was, admittedly, tiresome. All she really wanted to do was vanish onto one of those little islands in the sea, where Jordan could never find them. But they told her they could never truly disappear from him. He'd always find them. At least, until they had a warlock or more mages on their side to produce a strong enough shield, whatever that was.

"This cat-and-mouse game has to end sometime," said Michael, a red-headed vampyre. "We should end it *our* way. We should go on the offensive."

The others murmured in agreement. She knew he was probably right. She wasn't trained for battle, except for what they'd been teaching her, but they were. They would know how to plan and execute an attack on Jordan. If they went on the offensive, they could better control the situation and she might still have a chance to end this peaceably, but if Jordan found them first, her chances for that would diminish drastically.

"Jordan only ever has two others with him. We can easily take him down," Niko said.

"He only ever has two *with* him, but he can summon hundreds if he needs to," said Inga, their most recent addition.

And that's exactly what frightened Cassandra and why they kept at this same argument. She refused to take the chance of losing lives to Jordan and his minions.

"What if we devise a plan that prevents him from summoning any others?" Michael asked. "We could ambush him and he'd never have a chance."

This piqued Cassandra's curiosity. She finally raised her head and peered at the vampyre. "Do you have a plan that would work? One with no bloodshed?"

Michael squirmed. She didn't know if it was her requirement or just that she'd said "blood." The vampyres seemed to have adapted to their new diet of only animal blood—their solution to prevent them from harming humans—but they didn't particularly like it. They said the difference was like stale bread and water compared to fresh beef and wine, in human terms.

The werewolves didn't complain as much. Their diets had always consisted primarily of animal meat, except at the full moon. Their hardest struggle came then, when the call of the wild overcame their humanity. The vampyres had to restrain them all night long as they whined, growled and snapped, trying to free themselves to hunt down a human. For those three days of every moon cycle, Cassandra had to take Andronika far away and keep her hidden. Niko said the Weres had been easier to control last month. They all hoped they would eventually lose that wildness as their commitment to Cassandra and this life deepened.

"Well?" she asked Michael.

"Cassandra, my love," Niko said, answering for his vampyre-brother, "we can't guarantee that."

She stood. "Then this conversation is over. Again. I will not risk any of your lives. We are not large enough or strong enough yet."

She turned and headed to Andronika's side to join her in slumber, ignoring the rumbles of the others. She just didn't understand how they could be so anxious to go into battle.

"*Cassandra*," Niko's voice yelled in her mind. It was the only way he could grab her attention. She didn't particularly enjoy the ability to hear their thoughts, feeling it an invasion of their privacy, so she kept her mind closed to them. They had to yell her name for her to hear, just as Niko did again. She froze. "*You said your father called this an army. He said you would have to lead this army and fight. Battle means bloodshed. You must realize that.*"

This is not an army. This is a small group of battered people. We cannot take on Jordan and all of his troops! I won't risk it. Not yet.

"*If we come up with a foolproof ambush? You know we have to end this. Let's do it our way.*"

She didn't think it possible. Jordan was too cunning to fool for long. She'd been amazed they'd been able to stay out of his reach thus far. Which was why they *did* need a better plan, one that required confronting him and possibly ending his relentless chase once and for all.

She sighed. *You know what I want, Niko. You come up with a way that keeps any of us from getting hurt and allows me to talk to Jordan and I will consider it.*

She possessed what Niko called the "power of persuasion"— another gift from the Angels—and had developed it by converting the others. If she could use it to persuade her brother that she'd been right all along and he could still be good if he wanted to be, then she could bring him to her side and help him save his soul. She just needed to accomplish this without losing lives.

Chapter 18

Jordan sniffed the air. His nostrils flared. A smile danced on his lips. He looked at Blasius, his massive companion, and the vampyre narrowed his dark eyes and nodded. Silently, the two made their way toward the scents. Jordan found it nearly impossible to control the excitement surging through his body. After months of searching and chasing, only to come up empty-handed at the last second, they finally had the group trapped in a narrow crevice at the base of a mountain. Why had they stopped there of all places, such an easy place to be ensnared? He understood when he heard their conversation and his mouth stretched into a teeth-baring grin. He motioned to Blasius to stop.

"We've had enough, Niko," a man shouted. "This is no way to live!"

"It just takes time to adjust," Niko's familiar voice argued.

"We don't want to adjust," said a woman. "Why would you force us into this? We should have never trusted you."

"Please," Niko begged. "Please give it a chance. Cassandra can help—"

"Cassandra is the problem," the first voice interrupted. "All of her rules and requirements. No human blood? How are we supposed to survive like this? Don't tell me animal blood satisfies you. Don't tell me you don't still thirst. We're losing our strength because of it. We're *vampyres*, Niko! It's only natural to drink from humans. That's what we're created for!"

Jordan's grin spread wider. He had taught them so well the art of conniving and deception. He should have never doubted their loyalty. Glad to have them back, he took this as his cue. He signaled Blasius and they sped to the mouth of the crevice, effectively cornering the group of four—two vampyres and two werewolves. He was disappointed not to have Cassandra, but he was already working on that. She would join them shortly.

"You are right, Faiz," Jordan said, eyeing the black-haired vampyre. He'd been one of Jordan's more recent favorites. "That is what you were created for. And if that is what you want, we shall have you a human shortly. I'm sure you are *dying* of thirst."

Faiz's tongue slid along his lips as he nodded. "We came to her for you, but we cannot stand it any longer."

"You have done a fine job. You will be rewarded. As for you, Niko . . ." Jordan flashed, appearing behind his brother-in-law and forcing him to his knees with a shove to his shoulder. "You are the cause of all this?"

Niko didn't answer.

"He's been trying to convince us that we could find our humanity again. As if we actually *want* to be good," the female werewolf snarled. "And that . . . that woman—"

"Yes," Jordan said, "she's become quite full of herself. No need to worry now. I'll take care—"

"Sir," Blasius said, nodding back to the front of the crevice.

Jordan grinned. Erik, who took the form of a bear when not human, held a struggling young girl in his massive arms. Next to him sauntered in the little witch Jordan couldn't rid himself of but right now didn't care. He would have given her anything she wanted at this moment.

"Very good. Your mother will be next," Jordan said to the girl who reminded him so much of his twin sister.

Chapter 19

"MOTHER!"

Cassandra's head snapped up at the sound of her daughter's scream in her head. Her heart shot into her throat, feeling the girl's pain, and she jumped to her feet. *Where are you?*

Letting her mental wall down for a brief moment, Cassandra saw through Andronika's mind as her daughter looked around. She glimpsed Niko—his wide eyes staring at her with surprise and fear—as well as Faiz, Inga and the two werewolves. Gray stone walls that reached high above surrounded them and Cassandra knew exactly where they were—the crevice where they had discussed trapping Jordan. She had never liked this plan and now she despised it. Her daughter was not supposed to be a part of it. How did she even get involved?

Andronika gave her more images—a vampyre Cassandra didn't know, a man's burly arms across her chest ... and a familiar face with icy blue eyes and blond hair. *Oh no! He's already there!*

"Mother—" Jordan started but she closed her mind, not

waiting to hear the rest.

Flashing hadn't yet become natural to her but running still was. She sprinted through the moonlit floor of the canyon, weaving around the stone columns that reached to the sky, hurdling bushes and boulders in her path. She rounded the bend that led to the crevice just in time to hear Jordan say, "next."

Then a shadow darted at her and locked her into a tight hold. She opened her mouth to scream but a hand clamped over it. She kicked and thrashed, but the arms only squeezed tighter around her, nearly cutting off her air. The attacker grunted when her foot connected with his leg, but so did she. He was hard as stone. A vampyre. Then she realized it was one of her own—Michael. Why did he hold her back? What was he doing out here? What had gone wrong?

A rush of air blew in her face and the next thing she knew, they stood in the entry of the crevice, now packed full of bodies, only one of them human. A big bear of a man still held Andronika whose fearful look made Cassandra gasp.

"Just as I said." Jordan swept his arm out at her with a grin. "We meet again, little sister. Finally. I've been looking for you for ages."

Cassandra didn't understand his joy—true joy she could feel emanating off his body—when it was *he* who had been trapped. He and his two troops were out-numbered. But . . . why did her own followers just stand there? Why weren't they doing anything?

She glanced around the room. Niko's eyes remained on their daughter and his nostrils flared with anger. The vampyre she didn't know towered over him, his hand gripping Niko's shoulder, holding him still. And the others did nothing. Cassandra's heart sunk to the pit of her stomach. So much for their ambush. So much for their loyalty.

"Did you really think they would fight *me?*" Jordan asked her and her eyes cut back to him. "These are *my* troops, Cassandra. Not yours. You can't change Daemoni. You can't eliminate the evil that they are. It's in their blood. In their *souls* now."

No! she screamed in her mind because Michael's hand over her mouth kept her from screaming aloud. Michael—her first convert after Niko. Holding her captive.

She'd been wrong all along. They'd only pretended to convert. Had this been Jordan's plan? Her eyes swept the room again and a lump formed in her throat. She didn't have to listen to their minds—the truth was right in front of her. Inga's eyes danced with joy and a small smile curved her lips.

Inga, Cassandra could almost understand. She hadn't been with them long enough. She probably still had evil coursing through her veins, especially as she'd been born Daemoni, not turned. But the rest? How could they?

"They're *mine*," Jordan said, his face suddenly right in front of hers, his hot breath blowing against her cheeks. His icy blue eyes tinted red. "And now you are, too."

Everyone suddenly came to attention, standing straight and tall behind Jordan. Backing him. Everyone but Niko.

Father lied. I don't have the power to save them.

"*Don't believe it, Cassandra,*" Father's voice spoke in her mind. "*He lies. They are yours. They are God's. The Daemoni's most powerful weapon is deceit. Use the powers we've given you. You can win this fight.*"

Fight. Exactly what she didn't want. She'd accepted her powers that she thought she'd used to help these people, but she refused to use her powers to hurt.

"*You have to,*" Father said. "*This is why we gave them to you. You have to protect Andronika and the rest of them. You can do this, Cassandra. Listen to their thoughts and you'll know the truth.*"

I can't, Father. I can't invade their minds. I can't let their thoughts invade mine. I can't stand it!

"*Cassandra, you* MUST *do this. You must do it now. If Jordan wins, all humanity is at stake!*"

Cassandra's breath caught at her father's voice thundering in her head. She'd never heard him so angry and adamant. She felt his truth wash over her and it gave her strength.

With no time to probe their individual minds, Cassandra blew out a breath of resignation and let down her mental shield completely. She let the voices pour in. Andronika's screams of panic. Jordan's plans for taking them to the Ancients. His vampyre and bear-man impatient for their orders. Inga's delightful, "*Finally!*"

And the others all surprised her. On the inside, Niko was calm and felt in control of the situation. Faiz and Michael waited for orders, too, but not from Jordan. From her. The werewolves were just waiting for the word to change. Her heart leapt with hope.

She gathered the good force within her, pulling it all into a ball of energy in her chest. It charged and swirled within her and its warmth filled her with confidence. She prepared to unleash it.

NOW! She silently bellowed as she pushed the energy outward.

Chapter 20

Before Jordan could do anything, chaos broke out.

Michael freed Cassandra just before a burst of energy exploded from her. Blasius and Erik screamed like women. Andronika flew to the corner. Then Erik exploded into a bear, a rain of goo falling around them. His lips pulled back from his mouth to reveal sharp teeth as he threw back his head and roared. With two more messy bursts, the werewolves changed, as well.

As much as he wanted to see a fight, Jordan wouldn't have his troops battle each other for no apparent reason. They were all on the same side. He opened his mouth to deliver orders.

But then everything went wrong.

The werewolves charged at the bear's throat. Michael attacked Blasius, freeing his hold on Niko. *The traitors!* For a moment, Jordan felt a sense of pride in how well they had deceived even him, but he had to focus on the issue. He was outnumbered. He needed to act.

He twitched his hand and Andronika flew into his arm. He pinned her to his side and flashed outside the crevice, drawing Cassandra out.

She appeared several paces in front of him. He threw a fireball out of his free hand. She dodged it. With a tight grimace on her face, she threw her hand up, her palm face out at him.

Jordan tried to lift his own hand, but he couldn't move. What had she done to him? She held him in some kind of invisible grip, paralyzing him like a statue. Only his eyes could move as Andronika wiggled out of his stiff arm and ran behind Cassandra.

"We don't have to do this," Cassandra said. "We don't have to fight each other."

"*No, we don't,*" he answered with a thought, unable to move his lips. "*We can fight with each other instead of against each other.*"

That's right.

"*You and I together, little sister. We can do this.*"

Cassandra nodded. But he knew she wouldn't agree so easily, that she hadn't had a change of heart. What was she up to?

I can help you, she told him and she lifted her other hand. A low hum of goodness pulsed from her palm, licking fire at his skin.

He wanted to laugh. His eyes narrowed. "*Never. You come to my side, little sister. You can't beat me.*"

He flexed his own internal power, pushing back against her hold. Her hand began to tremble. He moved again. Her paralyzing power strengthened, but only for a moment. He broke free. His arm shot up, his palm held out toward her. The corners of his mouth lifted. He began to twist his hand.

Someone screamed.

And a blue streak of light hit Jordan in the chest.

He flew high into the air, far above Cassandra's head and then slammed back down to the earth. The air flew out of his lungs. Blackness flashed over his vision. *What just happened?* He lay still on the ground. His eyes blinked at his attacker. *Inga?*

"I'm not as weak as you thought," she said.

"No," Cassandra screamed, appearing at his side. She fell next to him and scooped her arm under his shoulders, cradling his head in her lap. "No, no, *no.*"

His vision went black.

But only for a moment. A bright light shone in his eyes, blurry and vague at first, but then it sharpened into an image. Although he hadn't moved, knew he wasn't in the real world, he suddenly stood face-to-face with Father. Father, with pants covering his legs, his bare torso crisscrossed with belts holding various weapons and wings rising from his back. Not thin and black, but white and feathered. Father opened his mouth to speak but a screeching sound drowned out any words he might have said. Then he was gone.

Jordan was back in his body. His eyes blinked open.

"Oh, Jordan," Cassandra cried. "You're alive!"

She still held his head in her lap, tears streaming down her face. She'd actually cried for him? She still cared for him, after all he'd done to her? And when she had been right all along.

"You . . ." He gasped. *How can I feel so much pain? I'm supposed to be invincible.* But he could hardly even speak.

She leaned closer to hear him.

"You . . . were right . . . little sister," he whispered. "About Father."

"Yes, Jordan. I know. And about us."

"No. Just about you." He coughed and she pulled back.

"You, too, Jordan. You—"

He had to make her understand just as he did now. "No, not me. You were always the good one. But not me."

"It's not too late for you. You can still join us."

He didn't know whether to laugh or frown at her optimism, at her unconditional love. Love—he realized now there was truth in the word. Father and Mother had loved him. Cassandra still did. Even Eris had felt it for him, he realized now. Perhaps he had even felt it for her. And the pain of not returning it for Inga— of his rejection of her love—had led him to this. The word he'd dismissed as useless actually held the most power of all.

How ironic that he'd been seeking revenge against all who had rejected him, while rejecting those who'd actually accepted him.

He'd been wrong about so many things.

He shook his head in her lap. "It's too late for me. It is."

"No, Jordan. I can help you."

Can't she see the real me? What I truly am?

He could feel her power growing, the goodness building within her so she could push it into him. His appreciation for her hope disappeared, replaced at first by fear that she would use her goodness on him and then by anger that he actually feared her.

The anger exploded. Hot, boiling in his stomach and chest. Strengthening him again.

He'd been right about one thing. Love deceived those who felt it, weakening them. The real supremacy came to those who didn't feel it, empowering them with a weapon against the ones who loved them.

He had no such weakness. He wielded the weapon.

"You can't," he growled. "My soul is gone, little sister. You can't save it. I've made my choice!"

Releasing his control, evil energy shot out of his body. Cassandra soared back several paces. Jordan sprang to his feet and charged at her. Too fast for her to react, his hands gripped her throat and lifted her in the air.

Chapter 21

Cassandra couldn't breathe. Her throat constricted and her tongue felt as though it'd grown twice its size, choking her.

Jordan, stop! I can help you!

"I DON'T WANT YOUR HELP!" he bellowed out loud and his hands tightened.

Her chest contracted painfully as her lungs fought for air. She thought her eyes would bulge out of their sockets. Lights popped in front of her. The edges of her vision swam.

Please, Jordan.

Her brother only growled in response.

"Cassandra! Here!"

She didn't know whose voice it was. She didn't know what came flying at her. But her hand reached out instinctively. Her palm wrapped around the object and she knew immediately what it was. Her hilt. Her dagger. The one Father had given her, specially made by his Angel hands. A grand weapon and possibly the only thing that could kill Jordan. If she could bring herself to use it.

How can I kill him? He's still my brother!

Tears stung her eyes, from the physical pain at her throat and the emotional pain at the thought of taking a life. Especially her own kin's. There had to be some other way, but she could think of none, except to let him kill her. Let him have the burden of murdering his sister. As he tightened his hold on her throat, she thought she had no choice but to let him. Her strength was drained. All her energy poured from her being as he choked the life out of her.

She looked for Father and thought she saw him through the shimmering veil. She wondered what it meant that she could see him—that she could see to the Otherworld. Was she dying? Was she already dead? And why wasn't he fighting? Why was there no demon?

"Your soul is already ours. The demons have no reason to fight me for it. You must fight for your life."

She had nothing left in her to fight with, though. The grayed edges of her vision pushed inward. Her lungs had already ceased trying to inflate and they collapsed in her chest. It was only a matter of seconds. *I'm . . . sorry, Father. I . . . can't.*

"Mother, please. Don't die. We need you!"

Andronika's plea came from a great distance, as if from another world rather than right behind her. But it was exactly what she needed to hear. Her daughter needed her. Her people needed her. If Father was right, humanity needed her. She couldn't let evil win.

And Jordan was nothing but evil.

How had she not realized this before? Why did she always deny it? She could feel the evil pouring out of him for years. He'd said it himself.

His soul was gone.

With a sudden and perfect clarity, she realized she'd lost

Jordan long ago. Years ago . . . since before Father left. The figure before her, about to kill her, was not her brother.

It was nothing but a demon.

And her purpose was to kill it.

She gathered every bit of strength she had left in her. She lifted the dagger. And she plunged the blade into Jordan's side.

His eyes widened at first, but then his mouth twisted up into a wicked grin. "You can't kill me, you fool. I'm *immortal*."

But his grip instantly loosened and they both fell to the ground. Jordan let out a single scream, mixed with pain and disbelief and rage. And then he fell deathly silent.

"There's only one way to immortality, little brother," she whispered, "and it is not the way you chose."

The skin around the silver blade smoked and sizzled, then began to disintegrate into ashes, filling the air with a thick, bitter scent that coated the back of Cassandra's raw throat. She yanked the dagger from her brother's body and watched as the rest of his skin dissolved into nothing and then his flesh and bones, until only his clothing remained.

She doubled over and cried. The sobs burned her battered throat and the pain felt right. The physical pain to match her emotional agony. The heartbreak that she and her brother had come to this. That he had gone so far on that other path that he could never return, even when he finally realized he'd taken the wrong road. She'd lost him many years ago, but only now felt the real emptiness.

She felt arms around her—large and small—and heard voices trying to soothe her. Andronika and Niko. They hugged her, stroked her hair back and shared their love with her. Love that strengthened her, that would eventually heal her broken heart and put her back together.

Chapter 22

The others joined them outside the crevice, their emotions pumped into a celebratory state. For they had won. They had beaten evil.

Cassandra finally stopped crying and glanced up at them. Her swollen eyes fell on Inga. When Inga had attacked Jordan with her magic, the witch's jubilant feeling of served revenge had blasted Cassandra. Inga had deceived them all, made all this happen for her own vengeance. Cassandra jumped to her feet and was in Inga's face in an instant.

"You did this," she screamed. "You led them to us and brought my daughter into it!"

Inga's eyes widened as she shook her head violently. Then she dropped her eyes from Cassandra's and stared at the ground. Her voice came out in a plea. "You know I can't create a shield. My magick isn't strong enough. They found us and told us Jordan had already beaten you and if we didn't go with them, they'd kill us both. I could have flashed away, but I couldn't leave Andronika with them. Not alone."

Cassandra pulled back and she stared at Inga, not knowing what to believe.

"It's true, Mother," Andronika said. "I told her to go, but she refused. She stayed to protect me."

Cassandra didn't look at her daughter. She knew she told the truth of what she believed. But was what she believed really how Inga felt? There was only way to know and Cassandra had to do it to ensure they were all safe. She listened to Inga's mind.

"*And to kill Jordan,*" Inga had added in her own thoughts. "*Revenge is so sweet.*"

Cassandra pressed her lips together and backed down. Inga was on their side—had even protected her, she knew—but when it came to Jordan, the witch also did, indeed, have her own motives. This was something she would need to work on with her group, because they had to be above revenge.

"We're sorry for deceiving you," Michael spoke up. "For making you think we'd deserted you. Since you were not keen on the plan and didn't want the details, you were unaware of the ruse to fool Jordan. We were always loyal to you, Our Lady."

She looked at each of their faces and saw their sincerity and their commitment to her. She didn't need to hear their thoughts to know.

It was her own fault. She didn't want to be part of their plan, didn't want to use her powers. She didn't want them to even have such a plan, even when she knew it was necessary. She should have stepped up to her position of leader so they wouldn't have had to deceive her. Deception belonged to the Daemoni. They had to be above that, too.

She would need to set rules. Killing had to be a last resort and certainly not for revenge of a broken heart. Deceiving was unacceptable, especially to each other. If she was going to lead this army, they would fight by her rules, those that felt right in her heart. And she knew she would have to lead them. She knew the battles had just begun. The Daemoni didn't have Jordan, but they had his son . . . who, according to Inga, was even more powerful.

The Angels had given her their gifts for a reason—not just for one small fight but because humans needed her and her army. Yes, they would have to fight again. They would have to keep fighting. But they would fight justly.

Faiz and the werewolves built a fire and burnt the remains of Jordan's vampyre and were-creature, the only way to ensure they didn't regenerate. Faiz had called them Erik and Blasius. They had names. They'd once been human. There were many more out there who'd once been human . . . who might be able to remember that and come to their side. Many souls out there to save and many others to protect.

She had the beginnings of her army. She had her family. She had love and a purpose.

"We need one thing, though," Cassandra said the next day after sharing her new rules with the others. She hadn't been able to sleep, unable to wipe from her mind the image of Andronika's terrified face when Jordan had held her. She didn't think she'd ever forget that. "We need a safe place for the innocent, for the weak, for those who cannot fight."

The others murmured in agreement but no one knew where. Niko, however, was silent, staring at the fire they sat around. When he finally looked up at her, his green eyes shone and he smiled her favorite grin. She couldn't help her own smile, though her brows pushed together with bewilderment. What could he possibly be thinking?

He came to her and took her hand. "Follow my flash."

Her eyebrows rose. She didn't like flashing, the way it sucked the breath out of her lungs or how she felt so dizzy and disoriented when she reappeared. She preferred to run. Niko knew this.

"Trust me," he said. "It's the only way."

She blew out a breath and nodded.

They appeared in the middle of a forest of cypress and pine trees. She could hear the crash of waves on a beach nearby. And not too far in front of her, she could see a line of white marble columns. Niko tugged on her hand as he walked toward it. When they broke through the tree line and into the clearing, Cassandra sucked in a breath. Her hand flew to her mouth.

A structure larger than she'd ever seen in her life loomed in front of them, taller than the trees and at least ten times broader than the houses she'd seen in the village so long ago. Like the columns in front, the walls were of solid marble with narrow windows carved into them. A large wooden door stood ajar in the middle of the front wall. Above the door, strange symbols were carved into the stone. Symbols made of beautiful swirls and lines, just like those that had mysteriously appeared just above her left breast shortly after drinking the potion. And now, she instinctively knew what it said.

"Ah-mah-dees," she sounded out. She looked up at Niko who stood by her side. "What is this place?"

He looked down at her and shrugged. "You said we needed a safe place and something in my mind told me to come here. Or perhaps it was in my heart. I don't know. I just felt the need to bring you here."

Cassandra stared at him, not believing him. Then she turned around, taking the place in, trying to figure out why they were here. With her keen eyesight, she peered through the trees. With her heightened sense of hearing, she listened to everything around them. She realized they were surrounded by water. They were on an island. And somehow, she knew they were on her island, the one she had wished to escape to when she thought all was lost.

"*Yes, Cassandra, your island,*" Father's voice whispered in her mind. "*We've made this place for you and yours. To keep you safe, to provide refuge for those in need. Take care of it, for many generations will need it.*"

Yes, Father, I will. I will take care of them all.

Cassandra looked up at Niko and grinned. "This is *our* place. Our new home."

He took her into his arms and swung her around, celebrating her happiness. She buried her face into his neck and pressed her lips against his cool skin. He tightened his embrace and she'd never felt so right as she did this very moment.

Epilogue

Andrew and Zoe both inhaled sharply when Cassandra plunged the blade into their son's side. They already knew it would come to this. Andrew had fashioned the dagger for this very reason. But expecting it didn't make it any less painful to watch. Andrew bowed his head as his daughter sobbed in the physical realm. Zoe turned and stood in front of him. She lifted her fingers to his face and brushed them across his cheek. They came away with a pearly, golden liquid on her fingertips.

"He did what he was meant to do," she said, her voice soft, trembling. He looked into her eyes and saw they were wet, too. He nodded.

"Yes. He served his purpose—a good purpose—and now he will harm no more." He gathered her into his arms and they grieved for their son. And for the challenges their daughter would still have to face. For her purpose had not yet been served.

Andrew remained close to the veil, always watching, always helping fight the demons for the souls Cassandra tried to save. He watched as she grew the Amadis, the Angels' army on Earth, pleased each time she persuaded a Daemoni to change his life around. He delivered the Angels' messages to her when she needed guidance. He gave her strength and courage when she felt depleted.

As time passed, he also watched Andronika grow into a woman, marry and give birth to twins—a boy and a girl. With a heavy heart, he watched as the boy grew into adolescence and started down the wrong path. Jordan's path. As every son would do. He knew why, but there was nothing he could do about it. God had His plans.

Andrew witnessed Andronika receive her gifts from the Angels. She aged back to the single point in time when her body, soul and mind were strongest and then he and the others strengthened her even more. She gained terrific powers, different from, but complementary to, her mother's. She helped Cassandra grow the Amadis.

It became large enough, with the many, complex issues of a growing society, that Andrew directed Cassandra to form a Council to give her guidance. Andronika and Niko sat on her Council, along with Michael and Faiz and even Inga, as well as others she'd come to trust dearly. They provided their diverse perspectives on law, control, freedom and war. Cassandra became a great leader and eventually, Andrew and the Angels only interfered when necessary.

In time, the Amadis outgrew the island the Angels had given Cassandra. Andronika established a second village in what became Italy and it grew, as well. Not all of their members stayed in the villages, though. Some traveled the world, helping the Amadis recruit new converts. Some isolated themselves, feeling that living alone, far away from humanity, was the only way to control their innate urges. Others lived in groups in the world's cities. Mages often grouped together in covens and some were-animals formed packs, dens and flocks, whatever was instinctual to their animal kind. Vampyres formed a new hierarchy among themselves. If sire and child both converted, that bond always remained strongest. Otherwise, hierarchy was based on what they began calling their third birth—their first as a human, their second as a vampyre and their third as Amadis. Some of the different kinds of unearthly children learned to live together and settled colonies around the world.

Once Andronika's granddaughter received the Angels' gifts—what they came to call the *Ang'dora*—it was time for Andrew to bring Cassandra to the Otherworld.

Cassandra, he whispered in her mind one Earth morning as she lay in bed in Niko's sleeping arms.

"*Yes, Father?*" she answered automatically.

It is time.

"*Time for what? You have something new for us?*"

Just for you. It is time for you to join Mother and me here.

She sat up with a start. "*I must leave?*"

He could hear the hitch in her mental voice, a hitch of sadness and despair.

It is Andronika's time to lead. You have served your Earthly purpose. It is time for her to serve hers. Prepare yourself, my daughter. It is time for you to come home.

Andrew and Zoe embraced each other as they watched their daughter say her farewells and prepare her own daughter for her new role. Andrew's heart grew heavy as Cassandra said good-bye to Niko, who had so faithfully remained by her side.

"When I first chose to stay with you," she said to Niko with tears streaming down her cheeks, "I feared the day when you would leave me forever because I knew I'd outlive you by decades or longer. I did experience that grief, when I thought you were dead, but here we are. I'm the one leaving you."

Niko pressed his forehead against hers. "I won't know how to exist without you."

"You will focus on Andronika, help her lead. You've been with me from the beginning, always there when I needed you. Now our daughter needs you, my love. Take care of her for both of us."

Andrew turned away, giving them privacy to say their final farewells.

"They will be reunited," Zoe said quietly. "Just like we were."

Andrew nodded but said nothing. He knew Cassandra's pain. He knew Niko's. He felt it strongly in his own heart and soul. But this was part of the plan. Niko would come to their world soon enough, but not yet.

When Cassandra ascended the Otherworld, Andrew welcomed her with open arms and wings. Then she settled in next to him, always watching the Earthly realm, watching Andronika and Niko and the rest of the Amadis, providing guidance and support when needed. And when it was time, Niko joined her. And later, Andronika.

Generations passed. The Amadis adjusted to the changing world and to the Daemoni, always counter-balancing their actions. At one point, it became apparent that the Amadis daughters—and the few sons—needed to be born and raised in the human world. The sons shared too many Amadis secrets when they were compelled to go to the Daemoni and, having lived their whole lives on the island, the daughters had become too isolated from humanity. It was decided they'd grow up in the human world, completely unaware that the Amadis or Daemoni even existed until they were ready for the *Ang'dora*.

These daughters married humans, diluting the blood and

powers passed on to their own daughters. A few times, Andrew, Cassandra and those who had ascended had to step in, discreetly providing a mage or one of Jordan's descendants as their soul mate. They only did so when necessary, though.

They watched the Daemoni, too. They watched their many attempts to increase their numbers before they were once again driven back by the Amadis and the Angels. They kept an eye on them as they tried in vain to recreate Jordan's potion, what Andronika dubbed as Jordan's Juice. They grieved for the souls of all the failed experiments. Then there was success. With a cup of potion, Lucas, a descendant of Jordan, became their most powerful leader since Deimos. But that wasn't enough for them. The demons and the Daemoni planned to create their ultimate warrior and the Angels made their own plans.

"He will be born here," Andrew told Cassandra, pointing at a spot on the timeline in front of them.

"But she won't be born until here?" Cassandra asked, indicating another point much further down the line.

"Correct."

"But why?"

"The Higher Angels have their reasons. The demons will be increasing the Daemoni's powers then. That is when they are needed."

"She must be stronger than these others," Cassandra said, running her finger along the names of the daughters still to come.

"Yes. Katerina will have your mind-reading abilities, but that is her only major power. Sophia's blood will be even weaker, but her heart and soul will be strong. She will mate with Lucas."

Cassandra's eyes widened. "There must be another way."

Andrew shook his head. "The Angels are adamant. They have it all planned. Lucas and Sophia's daughter must be a powerful warrior. She will face much bigger battles than even you did. She needs to be a match—and a counter-balance—to the one the Daemoni make now."

"But they will be together?"

"They will have their trials and tribulations, but they will be a perfect team. And the humans will need them. For if they fail, the Daemoni win. The demons win. And Satan will take his throne on Earth."

Andrew studied his daughter's face as she looked up at him, hoping she understood the gravity of the situation. Because Alexis Katerina would need everything they could all give her—the support of every Amadis ascendant, every Angel in Heaven. She would fight them at times, sometimes fiercely, but they must always be there for her. The future of humanity was at stake.

Cassandra nodded and then she smiled with understanding. "She will be amazing, won't she?"

Andrew grinned back. "Magnificent. Our most powerful daughter since . . . well, since you."

Cassandra considered this. "No. She will be better than me. Stronger, more powerful, more intelligent and wise. For she will have all of us and nothing can overcome the power of all of us together."

Andrew wrapped his arms around his daughter and kissed the top of her head. "Let us hope you are right, my daughter. Let us hope you are right."

They gazed through the veil, watched the Earthly realm as a boy was born to the Daemoni and listened as the Angels celebrated in the Heavens.

About the Author

Kristie Cook is a lifelong, award-winning writer in various genres, from marketing communications to fantasy fiction. Besides writing, she enjoys reading, cooking, traveling and riding on the back of a motorcycle. She has lived in ten states, but currently calls Southwest Florida home with her husband, three teenage sons, a beagle and a puggle. She can be found at www.KristieCook.com.

Connect With Kristie Online

Email: kristie@kristiecook.com
Author's Website & Blog: http://www.KristieCook.com
Series Website: http://www.SoulSaversSeries.com
Facebook: http://www.facebook.com/AuthorKristieCook
Twitter: http://twitter.com/#!/kristiecookauth
Tumbler: http://www.tumblr.com/tumblelog/kristiecook

Want More Soul Savers?

Stay up to date on the author's website and the Soul Savers Series website. While there, be sure to subscribe to the author's newsletter to be the first to receive news on upcoming releases, website specials, author appearances and exclusive giveaways.

SOUL SAVERS SERIES

http://www.soulsaversseries.com/

PROMISE (#1) – Available Now!
PURPOSE (#2) – Available Now!
DEVOTION (#3) – February 2012

Made in the USA
Charleston, SC
13 February 2016